from "The Lottery" by Lucy Sussex

. . . she scans the horizon for the yellow pulsing beacon of her time machine, safe where she left it on the prehistoric beach.

She sees a light — but the beam is paler, constant, and moves above the surface of the water. A Cambrian precursor of the flying fish, she wonders, not recorded in the Burgess Shale? Then she puts her hand to her mouth, realising that the light moves too fast to be organic, far less anything belonging to this prehistoric Earth. . . .

Now she can see below the light a craft bigger than hers, and stranger — like a vessel seen through a distorting mirror. Shipbuilding from hell, she thinks: from the hull up everything is alien. Where are the crew? As she wonders this, a mass she had assumed to be part of the structure moves. It is white, bulky, topped with a featureless round head — a figure not in the least humanoid.

"Who?" she yells. "Who are you?"

POINT

Altered Voices

9 Science Fiction Stories

compiled by
Lucy Sussex

SCHOLASTIC INC.
New York Toronto London Auckland Sydney
Mexico City New Delhi Hong Kong

Publication of this title was assisted by the Commonwealth Government through the Australia Council, its arts funding and advisory body.

A version of "The Lottery" by Lucy Sussex appeared in *Overland 133* (Summer 1993); "The Battle of Leila the Dog" by Rick Kennett was first published in *Eidolon 5* (Winter 1991); and "White Christmas" by Sean Williams was first published in *Eidolon 11* (Summer 1993).

ISBN 0-590-60365-5

Published by Scholastic Inc., 555 Broadway, New York, NY 10012, by arrangement with Omnibus Books.
SCHOLASTIC, POINT, and associated logos are trademarks and/or registered trademarks of Scholastic Inc.

12 11 10 9 8 7 6 5 4 3 2 1 9/9 0 1 2 3 4/0

Printed in the U.S.A. 01

First Scholastic printing, December 1999

CONTENTS

Altered Voices

9 Science Fiction Stories

Introduction by Lucy Sussex

All stories, however much the author may claim to be a camera presenting a slice of real life, give the reader a viewpoint into another's world. In the case of science fiction or fantasy, the worlds depicted are peculiarly imaginative, bearing little relation to reality as we know it (or think we know it). These are realms imagined by means of extrapolations from current scientific developments, or by pure fancy alone; they offer us the strangest yet often the most credible of otherworlds.

Some of the stories in this collection start realistically enough. Gary Crew's "Face to Stony Face", for example, describes a police investigation that soon becomes far from routine. Sophie Masson's tale provides an alternative explanation for the phenomenon of circles in crops, but what that explanation is proves to be entirely unexpected. Sean Williams' "White Christmas" begins with a deceptively ordinary holiday trip in South Australia, but finishes with the end of the world.

Other stories are alien from the start. "The Lottery" takes a small boat into a past remote beyond even the dinosaurs. Rick Kennett's story is set on a larger vessel, a spacefarer, and deals with a problem left over from our own twentieth century. In Isobelle Carmody's "Long Live the Giant!", a woman named Forever tells a story of death, and of fairies at the bottom of the universe.

What would you do if suddenly you saw a flock of burning sheep? Mustafa Zahirovic provides an answer in his "Everything". Or if you were trapped inside a computer program, as in Paul Voermans' "Malcolm and the Intergalactic Slug-suckers"? And what if science gave you a power of vengeance beyond your most megalomaniac dreams? Sean McMullen assures me that Megan's experiment in "The Blondefire Genome" is perfectly possible for a high school student – a scary thought.

Many people helped in the creation of this anthology: the team at Omnibus, particularly Penny Matthews; devoted readers Rita Hart and Perry Middlemiss; Margaret Wild, whose idea it was in the first place; and especially the writers.

We have here nine stories set in nine otherworlds, the imaginative work of nine very different people. Try reading them in your local McDonalds, or on the bus, and then see which reality – fictional, actual, not to mention virtual – seems the most convincing, the most real.

The Lottery

Lucy Sussex

Lucy Sussex *was born in 1957, in Christchurch, New Zealand, and has travelled widely. She writes in various areas, from children's literature to science fiction to the detective genre, and has an interest in rediscovering and reprinting the work of nineteenth-century women writers. She has published one children's novel,* The Peace Garden, *and another, for teenagers,* Deersnake. *In addition, she has published a collection of short stories,* My Lady Tongue & Other Tales. *When not writing or editing, she works as a researcher.*

Imagine a small boat on a prehistoric sea. Imagine also, within it: a complex sculpture, part metal, part translucent scoops and tubing, occupying the prow; amidships, equipment and supplies, including a diving suit to fit a small adult of the species *Homo sapiens*; and finally, in the stern, the time-traveller herself. She leans back idly, one hand on the tiller, as the boat moves through the shallow waters off the ancient continent Laurentia.

The motor of the craft is shockingly loud. There are few of the usual sea-sounds here – no gull cries, for the evolution of birds, let alone their ancestors the dinosaurs, and before them the reptiles, is millions of years in the future. The coastline behind the traveller is bare rock, in a state of volcanic flux. The only life on Earth is below the water; and it is mute.

The traveller considers names. Here she is, over five hundred million years in her planet's past, and the geological term for this era is the Upper Cambrian, or literally, Upper Welsh, after the location of the first rocks from this time to be scientifically described by her species. Thus an age pre-dating humans, pre-dating language, pre-dating nationalism, received the Latinised name of ancient Wales.

Sweating in the hot sun, she checks her location. Currently she is travelling above what will be called the Rocky Mountains, but which now are submerged in a tropical sea, close to the equator of Cambrian Earth. She glances around, looking for a line of breaking waves, and finds it – a reef, at the dividing point between a wide lagoon and the open sea.

She approaches the whitecaps, and at a break in the reef edges her craft through. Puttering cautiously along parallel to the waveline, she scans the dark, distant shore, then consults her maps and instruments again. Here is the spot marked X, her goal. She stops the motor, and heaves the anchor overboard.

The boat rests, rocking slightly, the only sound the soft wash of the waves. The traveller stretches, then moves towards the machine in the prow. As she does so, a splash, small, very close, makes her glance over the side of the craft.

What she sees is a small bug-eyed creature, the size and roughly the shape of a mouse, floating on its back just below the surface. "Sarotrocerus," she breathes, "brushtail" – for this life form was named for its long tail, which ends in a cluster of spines. As she watches, it flicks its tail, darting under the boat in pursuit of some smaller prey.

She glances longingly at her diving gear but returns to the scoops and tubing of the machine. Finally satisfied that all is in working order, she opens the drawstrings of a bag to reveal a host of small red balls, lotto balls. They are not marked with numbers; rather, each bears a pictograph in black, a silhouette of a strange, tiny creature. She takes a handful, three balls full, which she inspects for a moment, rolling them around her palm. "Waptia," she says aloud. "Opabinia. Wiwaxia." All three are named in Amerindian, from the names of mountains near where their remains were excavated. She dribbles these balls into the machine, then lucky dips in the bag, her hand emerging with a ball showing a spiky monster. She grins. "Sanctacaris," she says. "Santa Claws." This animal was named by a palaeontologist with a sense of humour.

When all the balls are in the machine, each a representation and thus representative of all the life forms known on Cambrian Earth, she hunkers back for a moment. She is about to replicate an experiment that took place on this planet over millions of years, in which a cosmic lottery, involving movements of continents, glaciation, and meteorites, determined which species would be fruitful and multiply, and which would decline and become extinct.

Imagine the tree of life, although the evolution of a tree is millions of years in the future. No, imagine instead the sponges and algae growing on the ocean floor beneath the traveller. They branch upwards from a single stem, broad at the base, then tapering towards a single leaf at the apex. There is more genetic diversity, more branches on the evolutionary tree in the water beneath the boat, than there is on the whole of the traveller's Earth, with its birds, fish, insects, plants, fungi, Uncle Tom Cobley and all. But, with time, branches die, the index of possibilities becomes increasingly more limited, trilobites vanish, and so do dinosaurs, until, 530 million years later, the range of species on the planet represents only a bare handful of those living and breeding in the Palaeozoic era, the age of the oldest life on Earth.

Can the outcome of the cosmic lotto be predicted? The traveller intends to find out, by asking her assemblage of balls and scoops: which species will dominate the future Earth?

The first stage is to discover who will survive the Cambrian era. She moves levers, presses buttons, and the machine hums into action, rattling the balls through the tubes, sorting and selecting by chance, naturally. Balls are spat out, to go into the draw for the next evolutionary round. She catches them in her hand before dropping them into the bag. Sanctacaris. Ottoia, a worm. But little Sarotrocerus, the aquatic mouse with the spiky tail, fails to emerge.

With a feeling of regret at the loss of that happy swimmer, she discards the other balls and moves on to the next round. Three hundred and thirty million years later, and the Palaeozoic era is ending, along with ninety-five per cent of the species on Earth. Only a handful of balls are still in the game. Triassic, Jurassic, Cretaceous eras pass, along with dinosaurs, therapsids (ancestors of mammals), woolly mammoths and sabre-toothed tigers. She has, in her palm, all the Cambrian ancestors of the life existing on her version of Earth, the Earth of *Homo sapiens*.

"Who will inherit?" she asks, and puts the balls through again. Only one emerges, and she stares at the form depicted on it, before saying: "Pikaia."

Her ancestor, her humble ancestor. She did not really expect a bizarre Cambrian alternative, like Opabinia – five eyes, and a frontal nozzle like the hose of a vacuum cleaner, except with fangs; but to find Lady Luck repeating herself, replicating the cosmic lotto, slightly shocks her. She soon recovers. Before travelling back in time to her own era, she has other work to do.

It is pleasant work, she thinks, as she dons her diving gear. She sits on the side of the boat for a moment, watching the sunlight on the waves. Then she dives down, following the anchor chain to the ocean floor. The reef is atop a submarine escarpment, and its vertical walls, some two hundred metres in height, are adorned with brightly coloured sponges and algae, an enchanted garden. Something seems to be missing and she realises it is the fishes, for vertebrates have yet to evolve. But there is plenty of movement, though tiny, for most life on this Earth is no longer than a few centimetres.

Most life, but not all. Something nuzzles her leg. She twists around, thinking of sharks, only to see staring malevolently at her the predator Anomalocaris, at a metre long the largest Cambrian life form. Imagine utter weirdness, odd elements of other creatures jumbled together in a surreal mix: a swimmer mantled like a ray, but with compound, stalked eyes, armed with huge spiny claws, and a circular mouth lined with teeth.

It circles her, claws opening and closing, and worse, that mouth too contracting, as if it munches her already. She turns to face the menace, at the same time trying to gauge whether it is alone or hunts in company. One claw grabs at her – she dodges behind the anchor chain, and Anomalocaris clasps metal for the first and last time. She now remembers a small speargun up in the boat, included for emergencies like this. Fool! she admonishes herself.

It lunges at her again, and she feints with one arm. The claws reach up to rend and tear her unprotected hand. Now she kicks out, her foot striking the monster in its abdomen. The force of the blow tumbles it head over tail almost down to the sea-bed, mantle flapping wildly. Then, stabilising, Anomalocaris beats a hasty retreat – it is a coward.

Wary of another Anomalocaris, she gazes around. The water is very clear, visibility good even at this depth, and she sees that the ocean floor teems with life. She recognises Opabinia, like a minute nightmare, and others, their forms mostly suggesting ragged claws. She swims above them for a closer look, and abruptly encounters a troupe of Marella, creatures like a cross between a trilobite and a lace doily. They balance gracefully on thin, delicate legs, their feelers and long feathery gills moving slowly, possibly even rhythmically, as if they are dancing in the ocean current. As she approaches, they flee.

She shakes her head, glances at her watch, then begins to search the ocean floor for a particular trail. The mud here is unstable, prone to slides, so she digs carefully. Even if her ball game replicates the cosmic lotto result – Vertebrates Rule, OK? – her instructions are to make *quite sure*. Thus she seeks her distant ancestors in the Cambrian mud. They are not numerous, but after an hour's work, her task is done.

Back in the boat, she sets her specimens carefully in the shade of the lotto machine and starts the motor again, travelling southwards along the coastline. The day is beginning to wane, and she steers tensely, checking her watch often. The nth time she does this, a faint disturbance passes through the water. The boat pitches, and an instrument by her foot beeps, displaying a tiny array of flashing lights.

She grimaces at these signs of a minor earthquake, recalling the sloping ocean floor back at her collecting site. A mudslide has caught the weird, elegant creatures, carrying them down in a roiling cloud to deeper, oxygen-poor water. There, by a million to one chance, the small, complex bodies will be preserved, soft and hard parts almost intact, within the geologist's delight her species calls the Burgess Shale.

She relaxes a little as the boat travels further away, into a region of Laurentia more geologically sound. It is close to the end of the tropical day when she stops again, and, taking the jar, dives down to the Cambrian sea floor for the last time. This habitat is less densely populated; there are no Anomalocaris, no Santa Claws; in fact, hardly any predators at all. An ideal location, then, to release an inoffensive herbivore.

She opens the collecting jar, and shakes her specimens out. The meek will inherit the Earth – and you could hardly get anything more meek than Pikaia. Two creatures like fat slugs fall to the ocean floor and immediately burrow into the mud. There is nothing distinguished or distinctive about them, except that down their backs runs the notochord, the forerunner of the spine. Pikaia are the ancestral vertebrates.

"So long Adam," she mouths. "So long Eve."

Above water again, she finds that she has missed the sunset, and tropical night is falling like a shutter. Swearing to herself – for once her task is done, her orders are not to linger like a tourist, but return to the machine that brought her here – she removes her diving suit. As she does, the moon rises, and she sees that its face is almost smooth and youthful. That is one wonder, but another is that, as the sea darkens, phosphorescence appears, patterns of light dancing on the water. She could watch it all night, but reluctantly she scans the horizon for the yellow pulsing beacon of her time machine, safe where she left it on the prehistoric beach.

She sees a light – but the beam is paler, constant, and moves above the surface of the water. A Cambrian precursor of the flying fish, she wonders, not recorded in the Burgess Shale? Then she puts her hand to her mouth, realising that the light moves too fast to be organic, far less anything belonging to this prehistoric Earth.

It nears, and she turns, frantically searching among her pile of supplies. Weapons, she thinks wildly, I need weapons – but the outfitters of her boat have provided her with only the speargun, of limited range, for they anticipated nothing larger than Anomalocaris. Nonetheless she grasps it tightly, standing defiantly beside the lotto machine.

Now she can see below the light a craft bigger than hers, and stranger – like a vessel seen through a distorting mirror. Shipbuilding from hell, she thinks: from the hull up everything is alien. Where are the crew? And as she wonders this, a mass she had assumed to be part of the structure moves. It is white, bulky, topped with a featureless round head – a figure not in the least humanoid.

"Who?" she yells. "Who are you?", but there is no reply. Water churns as the intruding ship alters course, silently circling her smaller craft – like Anomalocaris, she thinks, uncomfortably. Infuriatingly, it never comes within range of her spear, but still it is close enough for her to see equipment piled in it, of a function she cannot begin to guess at, and at the back a tank, of some translucent material, through which can be glimpsed traces of motion. For a moment a large claw is visible, as if – bizarrely – waving at her.

The bulbous head regards her blankly. She thinks now that the uncanny visitor is wearing a protective suit, with helmet and visor, but cannot be sure. The circuit completed, the craft moves briefly away from her, then stops. The sea water settles. Then the figure unhurriedly moves to the end of the craft, busying itself incomprehensibly – until the tank rolls over, tipping into her safe Pikaia habitat a full load of Sanctacaris and Anomalocaris.

Even before the predators hit water she responds, jerking the motor into action. With a great flurry and racket she speeds away, leaving a trail of choppy darkness in the phosphorescence. Her hair blows behind her, near standing on end. Not only humans can cheat, she thinks. Whoever they may be – descendants of Opabinia, Naraoia? – they're altering the probabilities, ensuring the succession of their own ancestral line once Pikaia is removed. I've got to get out of here, back to the time machine.

She glances back once, at the receding light, then forward, intently scanning the coastline. There, faintly at first, then shining more strongly, is the signal, *on, off, on, off*, of her machine.

"Here I come!" she yells.

As if in response, the light pulses brighter, then suddenly winks out. She stares, waiting, but the mass of land remains black. Aghast and disbelieving, she stops the craft and checks her instruments, drawing another blank. There is no sign, visually or electronically, of the machine that would have taken her home.

The boat rocks in the Cambrian sea, increasingly gently, as if lulling a cradled child to sleep. She sits numbly, then suddenly becomes aware of water at her feet. Glancing down, she finds light at the bottom of the craft, a shallow sealet of phosphorescence. Slowly it rises, covering her ankles. Simultaneously she notices the scoops and tubing of her lotto machine becoming hazy, indistinct. And now it seems that her hands are fading, too. She lifts one above her head, and the Cambrian moon shines through flesh and bone.

They've won, she thinks, whoever they are. Pikaia has gone, and without it I can't exist, not on Cambrian Earth, nor in its future. She feels no anger at her disinheriting, only a brief curiosity at the form the alien Earth will take. It soon passes, leaving her resigned and calm.

The boat is slowly filling with water, not so much sinking as dissolving into the sea. She thinks that of all extinctions, the Burgess Shale fauna buried in mud, the mass asphyxiation at the close of the Palaeozoic era, the meteoric deaths of the dinosaurs, this is the most peaceful end, probably better than her species deserves. Now the water is bath-high and she leans backwards, floating in light. From her extremities inwards, she feels sensation go.

A sudden plash sounds near her, and langorously she turns her head to see Sarotrocerus, surfing on the gleaming waves.

"What will they name you, little fossil?" she says, her voice no more than a thread of sound, "the inheritors of this Earth?"

It seems to be looking at her, although the real interest, she suspects, is the small fry darting around her diffuse, fading form.

"Perhaps they will name you *Ancestor*," she adds, and with that faint whisper, the last human speech on the planet, she disappears, leaving only a patch of clear Cambrian sea, and beside it a creature never to be called Sarotrocerus.

Afterword

Dinosaurs may be all the rage at the moment, but "The Lottery" is about another group of fossils, earlier, and to my mind more interesting. The story was written as a response to Stephen Jay Gould's Wonderful Life, *which describes the bizarre and varied fauna preserved in the Burgess Shale. After reading it, I wanted to go diving in a Cambrian sea, to witness the living Marella and Sarotrocerus, but, lacking a time machine, the only way was fictionally ...*

The story was originally written for a magazine which wanted 2000-word tales on the theme of "The Lottery". What could be more of a lottery, I wondered, than evolution? Subsequently, after reading the story several times to various audiences, I added 900 words to it, incidentally wiping out the human race. Other changes made to "The Lottery" were scientific. In between writing and publishing the story, research into the Burgess Shale established that the wonderful Hallucinogenia, which I mentioned in the first draft, had been reconstructed upside down, with what was thought to be its legs actually dorsal spines, and its tentacles legs. Science, in this instance, definitely proved stranger than fiction.

Face to Stony Face

Gary Crew

Gary Crew *was born in 1947 in Brisbane, Queensland, and still lives there today. He lectures in Creative Writing at Queensland University of Technology and holds a Masters degree in Commonwealth Literature from the University of Queensland. At present he is writing full time with the assistance of a Category A Fellowship from the Australia Council Literature Board.*

Gary Crew is the author of five novels: The Inner Circle, The House of Tomorrow, Strange Objects, No Such Country *and* Angel's Gate. *His picture books include* First Light *(illustrated by Peter Gouldthorpe),* Tracks, *and* Lucy's Bay *(both illustrated by Gregory Rogers). His short stories are represented in several anthologies.*

In 1991 Strange Objects *won the Children's Book Council of Australia's Book of the Year (Older Readers) Award, the Alan Marshall Prize for Children's Literature and the NSW Premier's Award for Children's Literature; and more recently it has been shortlisted for the Edgar Allan Poe Award for Mystery Fiction in the USA.* Angel's Gate *won the National Children's Book Award in the 1994 Adelaide Festival Awards for Literature.*

For reasons that I won't go into here, I'd been taken off the street and given a desk job. I didn't care that much; I shut my mouth and blended in. So when the Commissioner's secretary said I was needed in the Big Man's office, I was wary. Why would Isaacs want to see me? I'd been clean for twelve months.

When I went in he was standing at his window staring down into the street. He had his back to me. I approached his desk and cleared my throat. "Commissioner?" I said.

He glanced over. "Ah," he said. "Constable. Sit down, sit down."

I took the seat offered, but as I did he turned to the window again. He rubbed his hand across his forehead, lost in thought. The silence was so long that I wondered if he had forgotten me. Then suddenly he sat down at his desk and leaned forward. "Stone," he said, using my surname in an intimate way, "how long have you been with the Force?"

"Four years, sir."

"And how long have you been out there in the office?"

"Would it be a year, sir?" I didn't need to think.

He nodded. "And in that time, you've done well. Fitted in well ... never behaved ..." He rubbed his forehead again, searching for a word.

"Inappropriately?" I volunteered.

"Yes," he said. "That's it." He relaxed a little. He leaned back and looked directly at me. "And now, Stone, on the strength of that record, I'm asking a favour. Before I tell you what it is – and, of course, you have the right to refuse – you need to know that I chose you for a reason. You might not think so, but I notice. I see you out there every day. You're not much of a talker, are you. Not ..." Once again, he was grappling to find the word.

"Not sociable?" I suggested. I knew what the rest of the office brown-nosers thought of me. *Stone by name, stone by nature*, they said, playing their pathetic office games.

"Yes," he admitted. "But I'm a bit of a loner myself. And that's a quality I admire. Indeed, it's a quality I need in an officer right now. Someone who can keep a confidence."

"I'm here, sir," I said.

He clenched his hands on the desk top. "Yesterday a boy fell to his death from a third-floor balcony of the Grand Hotel. In itself that is a terrible thing, as is the death of any child, but it is not something that would usually come to my attention. Not ordinarily. The reason I heard of it at all is that my brother happens to be the manager of the Grand. In fact, he's Chairman of the Board of Directors. One of the principal shareholders."

"I see," I said.

"No." He shook his head. "I don't think you do. I'm not talking about some cheap cover-up here. It's far from that, Stone; far, far from that. I wouldn't stoop to that. The truth is that this is the third death from that same floor of the hotel in as many months. And none of them was an accident. All three – including that poor boy – took their own lives."

He paused to take a breath. He was nervous. This was

heavy going.

"Now, Stone," he continued, "you might be thinking that it's easy to fall from a balcony at the Grand. Or that it's somehow my brother's fault. Either way you would be wrong. There's a guard rail two metres high to get over first. The boy climbed onto a table. The other two, both men, used chairs. So you see my dilemma. It's not just a question of my brother's business interests being protected – although one hint of this to the press and he'd be ruined – no, it's more than that. Like myself, my brother has a deep concern for the welfare of humanity. It's a question of knowing what it is that made them do it. And why there? And will it happen again?"

I had no idea what this was leading to. But I was interested. I was warming to it.

"You know, Stone, you get all sorts living in hotels. All sorts. Malcontents. And believe me, strange things happen ..." He rubbed his forehead again. "But not three times. Not three times in the same way, from the same floor. And not all so hell-fired determined to die either. Especially when one was no more than a child."

There was a pause. I guessed that it was my turn to speak. I said, "Are the boy's parents at the hotel?"

"There's only a mother," he sighed. "And she's with her family now."

"And someone from here handled the case?"

"A medic team. And a traffic officer. Sloane. Or Slade. I can't recall. He was on the street when it happened. I've spoken to him. He's all right. I've led him to believe that this is somehow political and told him to keep his mouth shut. He prepared this report and brought it in this morning." He pushed a folder towards me. "I told him that someone would be down to investigate more fully. That's what I'm asking of you,

Stone. I know that you've had your problems with the Force, but now here's a chance to do something right. To make up. You know, we're all in this together."

"I understand," I said. "Thank you, sir. It will be a privilege."

"There," he said, "I knew it would be all right. But before you go, there's one thing. I don't want you going there in uniform. No need to advertise, as it were."

"I could go back to my flat and change, sir. Slacks and a shirt. Would that do?"

"Anything not to draw attention. And Stone, if you had to, could you stay over? To have a look around, I mean. Take a look today, and then decide. My brother will accommodate you. On the house."

"Thank you, sir. I appreciate the opportunity."

The Commissioner's brother met me in reception. He was a little man with a pink rosebud in his pin-striped lapel. "Isaacs," he said, extending his hand. "I'm the manager here. And you must be Constable Stone?"

He took me by the elbow and led me into an elevator. "I'll show you where it happened, then I'll leave you to look around."

We stepped out onto the third floor. "There are five rooms facing the street," he explained, jingling a set of keys. "They number 301 to 305. The first of our accidents, as I prefer to call them, was from 304. The next was from 302. The boy was in here." He slipped a key into the keyhole of 303 and the door swung open.

I'd taken digs in plenty of hotels over the years, but none had been furnished as lavishly as this. "I don't know if my brother told you," Isaacs said, "but the entire hotel has just been remodelled, inside and out. Nearly a million and a half, it cost us … me, I should say. But it was a case of have to. The local precinct has been re-zoned, and we either shaped up or pulled the place down. The building opposite is due for demolition in the next three months. Here, I'll show you outside."

He opened a sliding door and passed through onto a balcony. I followed.

The outlook was terrible. Directly across the street, hardly fifteen metres away, loomed a brick wall, its bareness relieved only by a pair of stone gargoyles: ugly things that stared back from dim niches set into the wall.

"That's the old Bijou Theatre across the road," Isaacs said. "Not much to look at, is it? That's the backstage wall. Very high. They used to fly the sets there. You know, hoist them right up. Been condemned for years. But come back in a few months, and you'll be surprised. After it's demolished – and that pair of monstrosities with it – the council's leaving the space as a park to show off St Mary's Cathedral on the other side. A sort of touristy thing. All to our advantage of course, hotel right on the park. Beautiful new outlook. That's why we redid the front in mirrored glass."

I was so taken with the gargoyles that he had to tap me on the shoulder to regain my attention.

"Here," he said. "You see?" He turned his back on the Bijou and pointed up. Other than the balconies that protruded from each suite, the entire street face of the Grand was glass; sheet after sheet rising to the top, two floors above.

"All you're seeing is the wall opposite now," he admitted. "But, as I said, come back in a few months when the Bijou's gone, and you'll see the full length of St Mary's spire reflected there. Beautiful. And cheap too. Very economical. We just mounted the glass over the old facade."

He would have gone on, but the time had come to remind

him why I was there. "That boy," I said. "Where exactly did he fall from?"

His hand went to his forehead – a nervous mannerism identical to his brother's – and he looked at the balcony railing. "Here, I think ... or here ..." He didn't seem to know.

"It's not a problem," I said. "If you leave now, I'll read the officer's report." My tone of voice offered him no choice.

As soon as he had gone, I relaxed in the lounge and opened the file. It included a transcript of Slade's interview with the boy's mother. In part, it read:

Mrs Parker had brought Aidan to town to enrol in the Southport school. He was to go there next year. Everything went well and he was very happy with the arrangements. He had been excited about going to Southport. They have a visual arts centre and he wanted to be an artist. Last night Mrs P and Aidan read and watched television; next morning (18 July) they had breakfast on the balcony. When they had finished, she rang for room service and the table was cleared. She locked the door when the waiter had gone. They were going to the art gallery that day. She went to take a shower and get dressed. The boy was sitting at the table on the balcony reading a book. When she finished in the bathroom she went straight into her bedroom and dressed. She called to him that the shower was free and to get ready himself. He never answered. At first she wasn't worried. He frequently ignored her if he was involved. When she came out to call him again, she saw that he wasn't there. She couldn't find him. She thought that it was odd because he wouldn't have gone out of the room in his pyjamas. She noticed that the balcony table had been pulled over against the railing. His book was open on it. She looked over the balcony and saw his body on the street ...

When I had finished reading, I telephoned the manager.

"The Commissioner suggested that I might check in for a day or so, to look around. Is that all right with you?"

"Whatever you think best."

"Into this room, if possible? Into 303?"

"Certainly," he said.

I rang the Commissioner and asked him to send over any files on the other two deaths. I told him that I would be working from the hotel, as he suggested. I took a cab back to my flat and gathered a few things.

That night I had dinner brought to my room. I sat on the balcony and ate in peace. I read the files over a beer or two.

The first death had occurred in 304, to my left as I faced the street. James Arkwright. Forty-three years old. Sales representative for a cosmetics firm. In town to accept a promotion to Sales Manager. Fell to his death at 9.30 am. Apparently stepped on a chair to get over the guard rail.

The second was Edward Enright. Twenty-eight years old. Architect. In town to promote the design for a condominium. Breakfasted happily with friends in the first-floor bistro. Fell from his balcony at 9.40 am. A chair was against the balcony rail.

I put together what I had. It wasn't much. Other than the fact that all three had died in the morning, there was nothing to link their deaths.

I opened another beer and sat back, listening to the sounds of the street drifting up from below. I stayed out until midnight.

I had breakfast on the balcony too. The gargoyles stared out, their mouths turned down, their necks and shoulders still in shadow. I offered one a coffee, as a joke.

As the sun broke over the Bijou I got up. I had seen the view from 303; now it was time to check the adjoining rooms.

I found Isaacs in reception and he gave me the keys without any trouble. "I doubt that you'll find anything there," he said, "but I've cleared the floor for you. At least, all the rooms that face the street. You can have 301 and 305 too, if you want."

It would do no harm to be thorough.

I went into 304 first. It was identical to 303, right down to the prints on the wall. But as I turned to leave the balcony, I had the distinct feeling that I was being watched, and looked over my shoulder to see the gargoyle opposite staring directly at me.

I went down to 305. The sun was well up by then, pouring down over the top of the Bijou, and as I turned in from the balcony I glimpsed the reflection of a gargoyle in the mirrored glass. I turned to look. It was staring straight at me. "Hello again," I said, and was about to step inside when I hesitated, realising something odd. This was 305. The gargoyle was opposite 304. It had been staring at me from there too. Directly at me. So, now that I was in 305, at least ten metres further to the left, how could its eyes still be on me? How could its eyes ...?

I shook my head. I was imagining.

I left the room and made my way along the corridor to 303. But as I put the key to the lock I reconsidered. I moved down one door. I opened 302 and went through to the balcony. The eyes of the second gargoyle were staring directly at me. I left the suite and opened 301. I passed through onto the balcony and stood at the guard rail. The eyes of the gargoyle were no longer looking straight ahead. They had turned towards me.

I gripped the rail. "It must be the light," I reasoned. "The fall of the light as the sun rises higher. Or the change in the shadow." That was it: the reflected light from the hotel brightened the niches that housed the monsters. It had to be that. Nothing else made sense.

To be sure, I repeated the exercise. I returned to 304, then 305. I stood at the rail. The stony eyes were on me. I changed position to stand at the extreme end of each balcony. The eyes followed.

I returned to 303. I stood at the guard rail in the middle of the balcony. The gargoyles were equi-distant, either side of me. The day before, when I had stood out there with Isaacs while he rattled on about the mirrored glass, those eyes had been staring straight ahead. I knew it. Now they were turned towards me. They were watching, I was certain. And there was something else. Between the lips of each downturned mouth, the tip of a tongue appeared. A pink stone tongue.

I rested for an hour, then returned to the balcony. The sun had passed over. The stony eyes stared straight ahead. The lips were once again fixed in misery.

I drew up a chair and sat down to watch. Except for calls of nature, and one fleeting visit from Isaacs, I did not leave that position for the remainder of the day. I ate nothing. I drank only water. When darkness fell, I wrapped myself in a blanket and watched throughout the night.

At first light, before the sun had risen above the Bijou, I saw that the eyes were still focused directly ahead. Though they might still see me – catch me in their line of vision, perhaps – they were not turned towards me. Not *looking* at me. I waited.

At eight, Isaacs rang to ask what I was doing. I said I would contact him. I returned to my watching.

At 9.10 the sun rose above the Bijou. I turned to see a band of gold strike the top of the hotel. I watched as it descended, growing broader and broader as the sun rose higher.

At 9.23 the third floor was touched with light.

At 9.32 I was rewarded. A smudge of grey appeared. Second by second it grew to form a misshapen skull, then a forehead, and then eyebrows – wild and shaggy – and then the eyes themselves. In the instant they appeared, re-formed by the light, they came alive: they blinked once, then stared about, desperate, searching, until they met – until they found the eyes of the other staring back in the mirrored glass.

I was satisfied. I went in and showered and dressed. I telephoned Isaacs and told him to find any building schedules that could provide dates for the renovations to the facade. I asked him for details of the ownership of the Bijou. When he queried me, I said that I was working on something. Finally, I asked him to bring me the keys to 203 and 403. He said that they were both occupied. I told him to bring them all the same. After that, I got a beer and sat on the balcony to watch the show.

Isaacs telephoned at 1.00 to say that he had what I wanted. I met him outside 203 and he took me inside, explaining to the guests that I was a tradesman. I went out on the balcony, and looked up.

The process was repeated in 403. From that balcony, I looked down.

I asked Isaacs to leave me and I spent the afternoon in 303, immersed in the plans and building schedules for the renovations. Later, I made some phone calls. In the early evening I slipped out to buy a torch.

That night I sat on the balcony and ate and drank in full view of my shadowy friends.

In the morning, when the sun was fully up, I left the hotel and met a gentleman at the entrance to the Bijou. Money changed hands and he undid the chains that secured the door. I took out the torch and made my way through the maze of stairs to the roof above the stage. I crossed to the parapet at the edge. I looked over, straight down the sheer wall of the theatre. Beneath me, protruding ever so slightly, I saw the perimeters of the stone niches that housed the gargoyles. I was in the right place.

I looked up. Directly opposite was the fourth floor of the Grand. I looked a little lower. At the third-floor level, on either side of my own suite, I saw the faces of the gargoyles reflected in the mirrored glass.

I never saw such a show. I never saw such games. They grinned and laughed. They winked and grimaced. They flicked their tongues and puffed their cheeks. They were mobile as flesh.

But as I watched, the sun grew higher; and, as it peaked above my head at midday, the mirror blurred. A deadening shadow fell the length of the building. The faces were no longer sharp and clear. I saw the eyes roll in fear. The features warped and faded. Playtime was over.

I returned to the hotel and ate. Afterwards I napped. When I woke up I showered and then telephoned the brothers. I told them to meet me in 303 at 9.00 the following morning.

That night I went to see a film. I saw *The Hunchback of Notre Dame*. Something a little different, I thought.

When I came back, I took a beer on to the balcony and trained my torch on the Bijou wall. The stony eyes stared back, unblinking.

Right on 9.00 the brothers came to my room. They were filled with questions that I declined to answer. They grew indignant, egging each other on, gesticulating behind my back, trying to intimidate me. I led them through to the balcony and told them to wait.

At 9.12, right on schedule, the band of sunlight started to

creep down the wall of the hotel. I asked my guests to turn and see it. They thought that I was crazy, and said so. When the faces of the gargoyles appeared, little by little, I directed them to look across at the Bijou. The fun began.

The Isaacs brothers gasped. They approached the rail of the balcony, craning their necks to be closer. They pulled the table over and clambered on to it, like children, leaning out further and further into the void. Anything to be closer, to see more.

They would have fallen if I hadn't grabbed their coats and dragged them back.

"Those are your killers," I said. "It was your renovations that gave them life; your mirrored glass that let them see each other for the first time. Introduced them after all these years. Made them social animals, so to speak. Let them come out to play. But not for long. Just an hour or so every day while the morning sun is right; and after that, well, once the glass falls into shadow, it's early to bed ... like good little boys."

Rubbish, the brothers said, making faces. Insane.

But when I showed them the building schedule and pointed out the date of the first death, the day after the facade glazing was completed, they listened.

"Why not any other floor?" the manager demanded. "Why only the third?"

"Because of those niches," and I indicated the recesses from which the faces stared. "Looking up from two, or looking down from four, you can see nothing; but at three, you are in a direct line of vision."

"What will I do?" he bleated.

I shrugged. The solution was easy. "Don't let the third floor front," I answered. "The Bijou comes down in three months, and then your worries are over."

"Three months," he howled. "I can't afford to lose my front rooms for three months ..."

I laughed. He had never cared about the loss of life. He would have let the rooms in a minute if there was no risk of exposure.

"I could have them closed for you," I suggested. "And perhaps more than just them." I opened my arms to indicate the hotel generally. "One call to the press ..."

The Commissioner stepped forward. "Close the rooms. As he says, in three months, they'll bring a fortune with the view of the cathedral across the park. We'll make it up ..." He realised what he had said, and was silent.

I heard. I had suspected. "We?" I repeated. "We? You're partners?"

His hand went to his forehead. "Stone," he muttered, "it didn't seem quite appropriate that you should know. I thought ..."

I laughed again. "Now it's my turn to do *you* a favour," I said, perching on the railing to face them. "I've taken quite a fancy to this room. I've never really had a home. Not a proper one to call my own. But 303 feels right, somehow. So I'll tell you what. You let me have it, rent free, and I'll consider this case closed. If not, I'll have the press up here faster than you can say 'suicide'. You understand?"

It was a strange thing, quite without precedent in city records, but the demolition of the Bijou was completed two months before schedule. I know. I had a box seat at the Grand. And when the dust had cleared, I went to see a gentleman who found the gargoyles among the rubble. They were more or less intact: one had lost part of an ear; the other had a chip in its shoulder.

I had them mounted on iron brackets, one each side of the

balcony door, facing out over the city towards St Mary's Cathedral across the park. I must say that they look good there.

But sometimes, after my second beer, I take them down and sit them on the floor, face to face. They like that very much, and play at winking and grimacing and poking out their tongues for hours. I envy them in some ways. I never was much good at games.

Afterword

Since childhood I have loved stories about bizarre discoveries of monsters, or exotic rituals, or unsolved wonders; stories that cross over between fact and fiction. Science fiction stories often use many of these exciting possibilities as their basis, and extend the imagination into fantastic new realms.

My story "Face to Stony Face" comes from an idea I had while I was flicking through a book called Nightmares in the Sky, *written by Stephen King, and accompanied by photographs by "f-stop" Fitzgerald.* Nightmares in the Sky *is a book about gargoyles: those fantastical stone-faced creatures that stare down on us from old buildings. I know that there have been other stories written about gargoyles coming alive, but I wanted to write one where modern science was the animator, not some whim of nature such as lightning, or a freak accident. In "Face to Stony Face", therefore, it is the erection of the new high-tech mirrored glass facade on a hotel that leads to the animation ... and the resultant deaths.*

The Battle of Leila the Dog

Rick Kennett

Rick Kennett *was born in 1956 in Melbourne and has lived there ever since (he hates to travel). When he left school at fifteen, he was already scribbling SF-ish stories in exercise books. He endured eight years in various engineering jobs, for which he was ill-suited, and attended the Terry Carr/George Turner science fiction writers' workshop in 1979. He left the course half way through, and published his first story a month later. Since then he has had several stories published in both UK and Australian small press and in several anthologies. Between 1985 and 1991 he hosted a science fiction show on Melbourne public radio. He became a motorcycle courier in 1980 and has not looked back.*

She took notice of it the second time in a spare moment after successfully tilting her donuts. She half turned in her seat and listened.

To the whisper of the air recyclers.

To the occasional voice.

To the low hum of the drive being tested.

Something had grunted, there at her feet; a sort of animal grunt, soft. She was sure she hadn't imagined it, not the second time. But all seemed normal in the Control Room. Activity was building up again after five days in subspace. Visual screens were still blank, but data lights were winking on the engineering, navigation and fire control boards.

Lieutenant Cy De Gerch looked up at Captain Brown in the command position. His eyes were on his data screens and scanner repeaters; he seemed not to have heard anything. Nor had any of the other officers and technicians.

For a moment Cy wondered if she were going senile at seventeen. She hoped not. It was Emergence Day today, and she'd have to be sparky when *Utopia Plain* hit the battlefields of the Procyon system in a few hours.

She peered at the space under her chair, as if daring it to grunt again.

The Captain's voice came quietly from her earphones. "Report manoeuvring status, please."

Cy tongued her lip mike. "Gravity donuts tilting correctly through their arcs, sir."

"Lieutenant Peters will take over the rest of the pre-emerge checks. *Chryse Plain* has just reported having engaged an enemy vessel in the vicinity of Procyon Three. Alter our final emergence co-ordinates accordingly."

"Aye aye, sir," she replied, but she slotted her seat over to Navigation with some misgivings. She knew the Coalition forces consolidating on Procyon Three were a prime target for enemy attention – a target requiring the heavy firepower attacks of a big ship. She began to compute a new exit hole in space, all too aware that *Utopia Plain* was not a big ship, and that even in company with *Chryse Plain* the odds might not improve greatly. And that was assuming just one enemy vessel.

Something behind her gave a low whine.

She spun about and stared down at the space behind her chair. She could see nothing there. "What the hell was that?" Her oddly pitched voice sounded harsh in the Control Room quiet.

All heads turned her way, but there were no answers. She realised then that no one else had heard it.

"Something wrong, Lieutenant De Gerch?" asked Captain Brown.

"I thought I heard a whine, sir. It must be a gravity generator anomaly," she said.

Whether or not the Captain believed this, he said, "Run checks on the gravgens and compensators, Lieutenant Peters. I'm not taking this ship into battle if the first 50g manoeuvre she does turns us all into red jelly."

Lieutenant Peters said, "Aye aye, sir," and went to work. But Cy knew he was wasting his time. There was nothing wrong with the gravgens. That whine had been animal.

And personal.

Utopia Plain emerged from subspace at the edge of the Procyon system, her crew at battle stations, watching and listening, finding nothing. Inwardly-rotating "donuts" of intensely focused gravity rippled down her hull. The donuts tilted and the ship curved towards the bright pinpoint of Procyon. Vanishing, she reappeared a second later millions of kilometres further in, where the frozen gas giants rolled. Again and again she skipped in and out of dimension, never in one place long enough to present a target: now cruising an asteroid belt, now passing the rocky middle worlds, now arrowing through the shadows of the warm inner planets, each time closing with the white disc of Procyon.

Cy had been too preoccupied to take pride in the precision of the ship's final exit from subspace. Although more important matters had crowded that weird whining to the back of her mind, it continued to push into her consciousness. It had sounded so pitiful, so *directed* at her. And the more she thought of it, the more she began wondering about that earlier grunting ...

"Contact bearing three thirty by twenty," said the electric voice from Scanner Room. "Range: ninety-five thousand and closing."

"Engage! Engage! Engage!" said the Captain.

Cy cursed her inattentiveness. There it was on her fire control screen: a shadow, a shape, an image. The target.

Cross-hairs centred, numbers flickered across her screen, ranges, bearings, speeds. "Forward lasers ... fire!"

Nothing happened.

For a second she knew cold panic, then she realised the

identification light was on, locking out the fire control system. She gritted her teeth. It had been one of the Captain's impromptu drills. The target had been their sister ship, *Chryse Plain*.

"Stand to," said Captain Brown. "Prepare to come about."

As Cy expected, the Captain's next words came through her phones. "Sloppy, Cy. Very sloppy. You've done far better than this in drills. And here it could've been the real thing."

She glanced up. Yes, he was watching her. "I was thinking about that whine. I can't seem to get it out of my mind."

"Gravgen running out of line. It's happened before."

"You know Peters found no such thing, Ralph."

"Then what do you think it was?"

"It sounded like a dog."

"Perhaps, Cy, but what do you *think* it was?"

She said nothing, only looked up at him again, and again there were no answers.

"Engage! Engage! Engage!" said the Captain.

Not caught unawares this time, Cy had *Utopia Plain's* initial laser pulses off before *Chryse Plain* did, hitting the enemy vessel they'd intercepted forward and amidships. It was a small ship, almost too small to be a concern for the planetary forces on Procyon Three. It was accelerating now, opening the range, gravity rings strobing down its hull. On Cy's weapons screen the image distorted like plastic, hard to keep in the sights. Laser pulses from *Chryse Plain*, seen as streaks of white light, flashed past it.

"She's playing hard to get!" said Cy, with a mad gleam in her eyes. The pitch of the drive's hum climbed. "Fire forward and starboard lasers!"

The ship echoed with the howls of the pulse-lasers. But the

enemy seemed to twist again, and only two shots found the target. *Utopia Plain*'s gravgens whined a non-animal sound as she accelerated through a one hundred degree turn. The enemy came back into the cross-hairs.

"Range still opening," said Cy.

"Close the range," replied the Captain.

Accelerating, *Utopia Plain* moved in, firing.

A million kilometres away *Chryse Plain*, also firing, closed in from the opposite direction.

Cy's screen was lit with thin white lines, raining towards the enemy. Then those lines twisted, bent themselves into sharp canine ears, the stars becoming eyes and teeth, the whole bulging from the screen like an animal snout. Cy, in her battle-frenzy, did not, *could* not see the dog's head pushing out at her – until it howled like the lasers howling through the ship.

She shouted, shoving at the thing, touching nothing, pushing against her seat-belt, pushing backwards from the console.

The guns fell silent. And in that moment of defencelessness the enemy closed at 200g acceleration, firing. *Utopia Plain* shuddered, and from somewhere aft dull thunder rolled, drowning out the incoherent yells of the girl thrashing in her seat.

Captain Brown re-read Damage Control's report, accompanied by pictures of the buckled superstructure shot by hull-crawling inspection cameras. He compared them with Doctor Norsk's casualty report of a couple of superficial injuries and a first-degree radiation burn. *Damn lucky*, Norsk had scrawled near the bottom. The Captain agreed. But it shouldn't have happened in the first place. Nowhere in the report could he find an explanation for De Gerch's behaviour. The only thing pertaining to that was the comment, almost an afterthought: *Lt De Gerch under observation*. He looked down at Lieutenant

Peters, now stationed at Fire Control. Peters was a good officer, sharp, thorough, the ship's next-best weapons officer. The only thing he lacked was De Gerch's genetically engineered empathy with the ship's fighting machinery.

The Captain glanced up at the main screen, seeing nothing but the stars. The enemy had escaped, forcing *Utopia Plain* and *Chryse Plain* to diverge into separate search patterns. For the moment all was quiet. But he always felt more secure with De Gerch at Fire Control. Losing her in that position was like losing a piece of equipment. What the hell was the matter with her?

He opened a line to the infirmary and asked.

"I can find nothing wrong with her, Ralph," Doctor Norsk told him. "Physically or mentally."

"Then why does she say a dog jumped out of her weapons screen, Ben?"

There was a long silence in which Brown could almost hear the doctor's shrug. "Look, Ralph," Norsk said at last, "she's a first-generation product of the Gartino Experiment, and after nearly twenty years we still don't know their full potential. Gartinos are still showing new developments, and not all of those developments are for the best."

"Are you saying that because of her genetic origins my second-in-command could go psycho at any moment?"

"No," Norsk replied with some impatience. "But there have been quirks and lapses before with Gartinos. I'd like to keep her under observation a while longer."

"Then you're classifying her as unfit for duty?"

"Yes."

"Ben, she's crucial to the firepower of the ship. That was little more than a scouter we fought. I wouldn't mind betting there's something bigger out there somewhere."

"If that's the way you feel, Ralph, then you can have her back. But first ask yourself if you can trust her not to see dogs again at a critical moment."

Cy sat on the edge of a bed in *Utopia Plain*'s infirmary, feeling not so much "under observation" as like a naughty girl confined to her room. She said, "Am I cracking up, Doctor?"

"Do you think you are?" he asked.

She hesitated, remembering the original grunting and what she'd thought at the time. "I'm not sure." She smiled briefly. "Isn't that a good sign? Doesn't madness always deny itself?"

"You're not mad, Lieutenant."

"Then what?"

"The mind is still largely unmapped territory. We know more about what's out there," he swept his arm around to indicate the universe, "than what's in here." He tapped his head. "Your being a Gartino may also be a factor. The effects of stress on someone like you are still unknown. I mean, here you are, the Executive Officer of a fighting ship, when most people your age are fighting acne. That must have some effect in terms of stress. But the question is: how does it manifest itself?"

"By hearing animal noises, Doctor? By seeing dogs leap out of fire control screens?"

"What do dogs mean to you, Lieutenant?"

"Nothing. I was born on Phobos, and although it's the larger moon of Mars, it's still a very small place as inhabited worlds go; so I grew up in fairly cramped quarters. No room for a dog, hardly room for a normal upbringing – if I can use the word 'normal' at all."

"Perhaps dogs represent normality to you. Subconsciously, I mean."

"Normality?" She slipped from the bed, paced a few steps

and stopped. "Just before leaving the solar system, you may recall we did a quick trip to Earth to pick up extra neutron torpedoes. While we were in orbit I had my first good look at the home world. Can't say I was particularly impressed. Although my family came from there generations ago, I feel no affinity with the planet. There's nothing of me there now. I'm a Martian, and normality to me is a small, red world with planet-wide dust storms, surface temperatures usually little better than freezing, and an atmosphere that's still being built. I can't see how dogs fit into that picture."

"Then why do you think you saw a dog jump out at you from the weapons screen?"

She sat down again and looked up at him. Once more there were no answers.

"Engage! Engage! Engage!"

Captain Brown was certain it wasn't the same ship they'd fought five hours before. It was still at extreme range, but he could see by his repeater screen that this was the big ship he'd been hoping not to find. At least not alone. He opened a line to Communications. "Give *Chryse Plain* our tactical position and celestial fix." He looked again at the screen. Yes, it was quite a big ship. "Tell them to get the hell over here at maximum acceleration." *She'll need at least twenty minutes*, he thought.

Down at Fire Control, Lieutenant Peters had the target nailed in the sights. "Starboard lasers fire!"

The image disappeared amid a smother of white streaks, then re-emerged, swinging left, swinging right, firing, closing, curving, dodging, firing, closing, distorting on the screen, impossible to follow, accelerating, closing, firing.

"Twenty degrees starboard!" said the Captain.

"Forward lasers ... fire!" said Lieutenant Peters.

In it came, hit and hit and hit, but still closing, still firing, large in the sights …

Lieutenant Peters yelled and instinctively covered his face.

Utopia Plain shook, hit.

Once.

Twice.

Smashed amidships, smashed aft.

Out of the rolling thunder came the whine of gravgens and the howl of pulse-lasers following the enemy as it slammed past. The Captain watched a report scroll up on his damage control screen – then forgot it entirely. Behind all this chaos he could hear the barking of a dog.

She floated, cramped in darkness, knowing only fear and loneliness. She'd been there a long time, shut away a long time, in the close dark a long time, round and round and round.

She padded metal floors, free and not free, really in that little dark ball, but now padding metal floors, free almost free like she had been in the sunlight, and she saw herself not herself asleep and she sat brushing the floor behind in an arc so happy, nearly rest at last, soft crying, waiting no more, leaping like she used to in the sunlight …

Cy started awake with the action alarm.

She sat up on the bed, feeling confused, training telling her to move, orders telling her to stay, while her mind tried to catch some elusive dream, fading, gone.

The alarm stopped, and in the little bit of silence before the lasers began to howl she heard that animal sound, that whining again, soft and plaintive, there with her on the bed, there in front of her, there where something was trying to form out of a milky cloud of no particular shape.

She leaned forward, staring. "Who are you?"

As if in answer her dream returned, vivid to her mind.

When the action alarm rang, Doctor Norsk was at his battle station in the surgery, taking inventory for the nth time with his two assistant paramedics. By the time they'd masked and had started scrubbing-up, the howl of the lasers had begun.

"Doctor Norsk, sir."

Norsk looked up from the basin. Lieutenant De Gerch stood in the doorway. "This is now a sterile area, Lieutenant," he said above the pulse howls. "Return to the infirmary, please. Either that or join the First Aid party if you feel you can ... "

"I understand the dog now."

"You understand the ...?" He gave his assistants a warning look, then checked De Gerch's telemetry readings on a bank of nearby meters. Blood pressure and heart rate were up, nothing more than battle tension normal. But brain activity was running riot. "It's probably better you return to the infirmary, Lieutenant, and rest. I don't think you're at all fit for duty yet."

"I'm not cracking up, Doctor Norsk," she said. "And I can prove it now. Ask the Captain to get a hull-crawler out to number one ion exhaust on our port quarter. There's a large spherical object lodged there. It collided with us while we were in Earth orbit and got stuck. That's where she is."

Norsk gave her a long, searching look, and wondered if the nerve of this experimental girl had finally broken. He made to speak, but was interrupted by the whine of the gravgens, unusually violent. *Utopia Plain* was manoeuvring for her life.

"How do you know of this spherical object?" he asked, using his best bedside manner.

"The dog showed me ..." She shook her head in frustration, then slowly said, "I saw it up here." She tapped her forehead.

After nearly twenty years we still don't know their full potential ... He remembered saying that not five hours before.

"Oh, Doctor, please! Let me go back!"

Whether it was the urgency of her tone, the pleading in her eyes, or some idea that she was indeed telling the truth, he suddenly heard himself saying, "Return to duty."

"Thank you!" She laughed and spun about, and in that brief moment Norsk saw in her the little girl she had never been. Then she was gone, and with her – he could've sworn he saw – the blur scampering at her heels.

"Range: eight hundred thousand and opening ... target coming about to port."

The Captain barely heard the voice from Scanner Room, barely comprehended the report on his damage control screen. He listened again for the dog, but it was gone.

On his repeater screen the enemy ship was curving through a million-kilometre arc, its tilted gravity rings distorting starlight into flares and patterns. Brown looked again at the damage control read-out: damage to Manoeuvring, to Engineering, to hull frames which didn't look able to stand another attack. He checked his repeater, then glanced in Lieutenant Peters' direction, wondering. As he opened a line to the Torpedo Room he noticed the flashing call-light on Surgery's line. He gave orders to his torpedo people first, then answered the doctor. By that time the enemy was closing again.

Hunched over the weapons screen, Peters noted with apprehension the winking of the Torpedo Ready lights. They were the weapons the underdog used when things looked desperate. Then, suddenly, there was no more time for worry or doubt.

"Target range nine hundred thousand," said Scanner Room.

"Closing at 100g acceleration … 120g … 140g … Range now eight hundred thousand and closing …"

"Permission to relieve you, Lieutenant Peters."

He jerked about and stared with open-faced surprise at Cy De Gerch standing beside him. He glanced up at the Captain, who simply nodded and pointed to the torpedo control panel.

"… seven fifty thousand and closing …"

Peters quickly unbuckled his seat-belt and vacated the chair, trying not to show his confusion and utter relief.

" … seven hundred thousand and closing … "

De Gerch adjusted her head-set. "Stand by aft tubes, Lieutenant Peters. Half speed, wide spread … fire! Forward tubes, full speed, medium cluster … fire!"

Soundless seconds later, eight spreading lines etched across her screen, intersected the following moment by eight more diverging from the opposite direction.

"Target taking evasive action …"

Peters glanced at De Gerch. She didn't seem to be listening to Scanner Room at all, and her breathing came shallow and rapid in his earphones. Captain Brown, watching his weapons repeater, saw the cross-hairs leave the target, go hunting across the screen. Frowning, he leaned forward, cold with doubt.

"Range six hundred thousand and closing."

"Stand by port lasers," said Lieutenant De Gerch, distant and choppy.

What the hell is she doing? thought the Captain. She didn't seem to be watching her screen at all, but simply staring straight ahead. He opened a line to her, heard her panting, "Be patient, little one … Be patient … "

He switched off, suddenly scared.

The enemy began to fire.

On the screen the cross-hairs veered to a point ahead of the target. Lieutenant De Gerch said, "Detonate first salvo!" and then, "Starboard lasers fire!"

"Target hit by torpedo!" said Scanner Room.

The lasers howled.

An instant before the target disappeared inside a smother of detonations, Captain Brown saw it shoved into the cross-hairs by the torpedo hit. Then all was chaos and the howl of the lasers going and going. Lieutenant De Gerch yelled once as the target area swelled and swelled, a glowing circle engulfing half the screen – then faded, thinning, gone, leaving nothing.

She slumped in her seat, head lolled back, wet with sweat, breathing slowing again, consciousness coming back to her staring eyes.

Captain Brown looked down at her from the command position, shocked by the realisation of how literally true it was that he'd thought of her as a piece of fire control equipment – an integral part of the ship's capacity for destruction.

Over the next four days *Utopia Plain*, in company with *Chryse Plain*, decelerated gingerly at 30g while hull-crawlers made patchwork repairs to the damage. During these operations engineers, led by Lieutenant De Gerch, found a large metallic sphere lodged in an ion exhaust on the port quarter. Brought inboard, it proved to be an ancient satellite which had apparently collided with the ship while in Earth orbit. They cut an opening, but it was Cy De Gerch who insisted she alone should crawl in to remove what she knew to be there.

It was a sombre trio who gathered around the hole dug deep into the soil of the windy grassland. The sky was blue and peacefully empty. The planet was now secure, and the fighting was gradually moving away from Procyon Three. Out of a sense of occasion all three wore their formal uniforms.

Cy lowered the little bundle of mummified remains into the hole. "Goodbye, Leila. It's not Earth exactly, but it's rest at last." She stepped back to allow Captain Brown and Doctor Norsk to fill in the grave.

By identifying the satellite and tracing it through historical records it was found to have been launched at the dawn of the Space Age, carrying a dog named Leila into orbit. But in those early days there'd been no way home, and Leila, after a week of orbiting, had died. Thirst? Suffocation? Loneliness? It wasn't clear.

With the burial complete the three stood looking at each other, feeling awkward. Far above, *Utopia Plain* was orbiting, being readied to join a concerted thrust into enemy space. The men turned and made their way back to the shuttlecraft, but Cy stayed a moment to place a flower on the little grave. She felt the heat of the day, smelt the green of the grass, and listened to the wind; listened with a kind of envy as it carried away the distant, happy barking of a dog.

Afterword

Why do I write science fiction? The glib, though honest, answer would be "I don't know." The writing urge swings in me from despair to compulsion and back again. Science fiction is a genre I feel comfortable with, though my forte is the supernatural. An aspect of this is time, and time fascinates me. But why? The answer to that may be the same as the answer to why I write science fiction ...

The characters in this story – Cy and her colleagues – came from a novel I self-published in 1981. It was basic space opera, as is "The

Battle of Leila the Dog" in essence. But, having since drifted into writing supernatural stories, I thought: why not throw something as wispy as a ghost into this slam-bam super science world and see what happens.

Leila was inspired by the Russian dog Laika, who became the first animal in space when she was rocketed into orbit inside Sputnik 2 on 3 November 1957. It was a one-way trip, and she died when her oxygen ran out a week later. But Sputnik 2 came down several years ago and burnt up in the atmosphere, so Leila cannot be Laika: she is a fictitious dog in a fictitious satellite.

Long Live the Giant!

Isobelle Carmody

Isobelle Carmody *was born in Wangaratta and moved to Melbourne soon afterwards. The eldest of eight children, she began her first book,* Obernewtyn, *while still at secondary school. She studied Philosophy and Drama at University, then worked as a features journalist and later as a radio interviewer.* Obernewtyn, *and its sequel,* The Farseekers, *were both shortlisted for the CBC Book of the Year Award in the Older Readers category, while her third book,* Scatterlings, *won the Talking Book of the Year Award. Her most recent novel,* The Gathering, *was joint winner of the Children's Literature Peace Prize in 1993.*

You! Come over here. I want to tell you the story of death and of the fairies at the bottom of the universe.

My name is Forever.

No you will not get into trouble for listening to me. Student groups are always brought to this wing because I am here and they think I am harmless. Like a friendly bear in the zoo, which will permit itself to be petted. The nurses are happy to have me to amuse those who come through, for it leaves them free to do their hair or call their boyfriends. They think that I am tame, but they are wrong. Oh you need not be afraid that I will bite or froth at the mouth or tear my clothing off and caper naked before you. But I am dangerous just the same because I may cause you to think too much. You can die of that.

Oh yes you can die of anything – of lonesomeness or homesickness, of a broken heart. You can even die of stupidity. And in the end, if you haven't died of anything else, you die of life.

Yes you are right. I am old and I talk too much. I will take your advice and get on with my story.

Is it a true story? Forgive me smiling. I know it looks as if I am laughing at you, but I am only amused by the irony of your question, for once my mother asked it of me in that same suspicious way. Or not quite. Her exact words were: Is that true or is it a story? You see how she used the word *story* as if it were the word *lie*?

I had told her, you see, that I was late home because the fairies had got hold of me and kept me prisoner. I created that story to make amends for having come home so late. I had not meant to deceive her so much as to offer her my story as a gift, little knowing how prophetic it was. The truth seemed a drab sparrow of a thing, and so I brought her a gorgeous plumed exotic instead.

She slapped me, and in the pain of that slap was an important lesson: No matter how wondrous a story is, if there is no truth in it, it is ugly. But truth is complex and rarely comes in the form of undiluted fact. Stories are facts with soul, and stories that have no truth in them are indeed lies.

The nurses here call me a liar you know. They say: The woman in Room 304 tells lies. Just as they say of the woman in Room 303: *She has Alzheimers.* (She is dying of forgetfulness, I tell children, and they nod their little tousled heads with a wisdom that humbles me.)

Why am I here? I suppose you could say that what ails me is the opposite of what ails the woman in the next room. I am dying of too much knowledge. I am distended with truth, bloated with stories, while the woman in Room 303 is almost an empty husk, the knowledge of her life all bled out of her. I have told her many a story to try to nourish her shrivelled soul, but they leak out of her as fast as I put them in.

The nurses would probably tell you I am dying of lies, which they call senility, or of old age. Lies do come easier as death approaches. They form a barricade against the tidal wave of fear that roars at me when I think of dying. Behind that flimsy barricade, life is piercingly sweet.

Stories give me the courage I need to keep my promise, and to laugh. I will tell you later of the promise.

My grandfather was a liar, you know. *She probably gets it from your father*, my mother used to whisper to my father, as if lies were hereditary. *Perhaps she is a throwback*, my father had responded, to dissociate himself from our bad blood.

My grandfather liked to answer questions with stories. *How can she learn if you tell her such outrageous things?* my mother would ask him in exasperation.

When a drunk driver annihilated my grandfather on a wet road one night, my mother shook her head and said it was a pity, but in her eyes I saw a certain satisfaction, as if he had got his just deserts.

One of the stories my grandfather told was this:

We were passing the city cemetery. Adjoining it was a field occupied only by a couple of amiable and motheaten horses, and a grey tower. I asked what the tower was for. My grandfather answered that it held a giant's arm.

(I have told this more than once before. But I cannot tell *this* story without it. It shapes the two great preoccupations of my life – truth and death.)

In answer to the clamour of questions this tantalising titbit about the giant evoked, my grandfather explained that some eons past, humans had stumbled on a giant's body in a field during a cross-country trek. *In those days this area*, my grandfather had said in a dry aside, *was completely deserted*. This accounted for no one knowing the giant existed or noticing the body sooner.

Human doctors came to examine the enormous corpse and found that the giant had died stretched out flat, except for one arm. Rigor mortis had set in, and the arm was fixed in that position. The doctors could not shift death from his bones long enough to lower it, and even the engineers and builders had no luck at it. Finally it was decided to bury the giant normally, except for the offending arm, which would be encased in a stone tower.

This would also serve as his monument.

I do not know if it still exists. I never leave this place now. As a young woman I would avoid the cemetery and the field with its mysterious tower. It frightened me, that monument to death. But now, when I am afraid and my courage fails, I picture it in my mind and whisper: *Long live the giant!*

Oh I was afraid of death after my grandfather died. I loved him and his loss grieved me. But the thought of him mouldering under the ground with the worms in his eyes haunted me. It drove me to seek out truth, for I had got it into my head that truth would save me from death – that somehow truth and immortality were the same thing.

Yes I am laughing, but I am not so far from sorrow or terror. I laugh to give myself the courage to keep faith with the giant. I laugh because truth is a wild beast with teeth that rend.

I abandoned the magic and fairytales of girlhood to investigate the source of life in a search for truth that would fill my every waking hour. When the test tubes and chemical equations of my prime yielded no answers, I turned in grey-haired middle age to philosophy. I was called wise and brilliant, but let me tell you, what lay at the bottom of all that studying and thinking and talking up a storm was my fear of dying.

At the last, I made up my mind to take the initiative with death instead of having it stalk me through the years. I was tired of waiting and it had come to me that perhaps death and truth were the same thing.

I walked out the front door of my house to the nearest bridge and jumped without bothering to leave a note or think twice.

One minute I was flying through the air towards the cold

and stinking river with its rotted black teeth of stone; the next I was hovering in the air, surrounded in golden light.

The fairies had got me after all.

Oh listen. That is not the end and it is rude of you to turn away when the going is rough. A story is a road and you have your feet upon this one. Kindly walk it to the end. This is the hardest bit, I promise you. It's all downhill from here.

Now where was I? Oh yes, flying through the air and then – floating. For a minute I thought I was dead and truly it was something of an anticlimax. I had been taken up by a molecular refracter, though you might as well call it a fairy dust. I woke naked in a cage of woven sunbeams, neither dead nor even mortally wounded. I was pretty shocked I can tell you. Nothing had prepared me for this turn of events.

The creatures who had got hold of me were humanoid: their heads were devoid of hair, but they possessed two great chilly liquid eyes, two slightly pointed ears, flattish noses and lipless mouths. They were much bigger than we are – as big as a two-storey building. Truly giants. We talk of giants, but you can't imagine what it was like seeing their great faces peering in at me, their pores open like little gasping mouths. I fainted straight away and several more times until I got used to the sight of them. And even when I began to study them, I could not like their hugeness for it dwarfed and utterly diminished me.

It was some time before I looked at them well enough to note that they were different in another aspect from humans. *They had wings*. Not glorious enormous feathered things such as medieval angels might wear, nor even gleaming transparent wings of butterfly gauze, or I should have noticed them sooner. Their poor shrivelled little wings of flesh had forgotten how to flap.

Seeing the wings, in spite of their smallness and weakness, I understood that what I had said to my mother all those years ago had come to pass. Fairies had indeed got hold of me, though they did not call themselves Fairy but Vaeri.

There was no visible way of differentiating male Vaeri from female, though I was told later that there were male and female. They were telepathic, though often they spoke aloud as well. They moved in a languid, sinuous way that always reminded me of seaweed waving in slow motion under the ocean.

The biggest difference between our races, though, was not their size, or their wasted wings, but their agelessness. It was impossible to say from their faces if the Vaeri were young or old, yet their eyes seemed immeasurably ancient. When I understood that they were immortals I gave up lethargy and disbelief and began to try to communicate with my keeper, wondering if here, at last, I should find truth.

Of all the Vaeri, my keeper alone seemed able to display emotion, and at first this was so subtle as to be imperceptible. Gradually I became aware that he was pleased when I responded to his overtures. He was the only one of that giant race who tried to reach me with words and pats and small fumbling kindnesses. His name was Borth Jesu H and he named me Awen-du.

I learned the language of my captors with extraordinary rapidity, and only later understood that the potential for this language, indeed the memory of it, was buried in my genetic make-up. At the time I thought it was my own brilliance that enabled communication with these alien beings.

My life among the Vaeri fell swiftly into routine. There would be great periods of time when Borth would ask me about my life. In particular, about my suicide attempt. I was more interested in finding out if the stories of fairies on Earth had been planted by his people, and what it was to be immortal. He always managed to turn the topic to his own questions, though. If I asked too persistently where I was, or why, or even how I had got there, he would simply go away and leave me alone.

In between our long conversations and being fed the tasteless paste which Borth said cost much effort to prepare, I would be bathed in ion rays that separated all grime from my flesh, and taken to an enormous room with a great vaulted ceiling open to the stars. This was a sort of circular amphitheatre around which sat rank upon rank of white-robed Vaeri facing a small central stage where I was made to stand.

My first trips to this room were frightening simply because I was afraid I was to be killed and eaten, or sacrificed.

But no one even addressed me, though the speakers would often point at me. As I learned their language I came to understand that the word they called me, Uman, meant monster. Once it would have mortified me to be called that, but since the Vaeri themselves could not help being aware of my likeness to them, I assumed it could not be my form in general that repulsed them.

I know now that this likeness of human to Vaeri was the very thing that made me a monster to them. Then, I decided it must have been the result of some action of mine. And since they had taken me from my suicide, I decided I must be on trial for that, for I had become convinced this was some sort of galactic enquiry.

"You are not on trial," Borth had assured me when I asked.

Humanity then? I had guessed, but he would not answer. I decided that must be it – Earth was on trial and I was an example of my race. Poor Earth, I thought.

I did not understand the trial procedure at all. Individuals of the Vaeri spoke in a sort of high oratory when they addressed those gathered in the dome, and their words were so abstract as to be nonsense.

These alien rites were fascinating to begin with, then dull, then worrying; for as time passed, I began to fear for my own fate. Whether I was on trial or not, this strange enquiry centred somehow on me.

Why, you might reasonably ask, should someone who had been quite content to abandon life altogether be concerned about anything that happened thereafter? But now that life was forced on me, I had rediscovered an interest in it.

The end of the trial came quite without warning. One day Borth did not come, and another Vaeri brought me to the dome. Then Borth was brought there also and stood beside me. I had not previously thought of him as anything but my keeper, but now I saw that I had been wrong.

"You, Borth Jesu H, chosen above many to study Creation, are charged with creating monsters," said one of the Vaeri.

I was shocked to realise it was Borth who was on trial. But the mention of monsters puzzled me greatly. The Vaeri had called me a monster – were they saying Borth had created me?

I did. Borth sent the words to my mind. I realised he had taken the question from my thoughts.

"I do not believe my creations are monsters," Borth said aloud. "How could they be when I modelled them upon our own forms?"

"You admit you made images of the Vaeri from Murmi clay, always intending to breathe life into them?"

"I did," Borth said. "I do not regret it."

What is Murmi? I thought loudly, hoping Borth would hear.

I hear, he sent.

Then he told me this, in thought, so it came to me swiftly:

There are many sorts of clay. At first, students of Creation are given Ramo to practise on – a coarse and short-lived clay which will hold no life. This is intended to develop dexterity and aesthetic taste. In time, we progress to Pya, a softer, finer clay that allows greater subtlety of form and develops delicacy of touch and restraint. Everything created of these clays is destroyed lest something imperfect accidentally be given lifebreath.

Only in the final stages of study are students permitted the use of Murmi, an actual form of Porsoul. Of all the clays, only these two are dense and complex enough to contain and hold sentient life. Murmi starts out as Porsoul, but at some point before maturity, it is flawed and begins to decay. Use of it gives the students a feel for the real thing, but its flaw prevents it keeping hold of lifebreath. Whatever is formed of it will degenerate as the lifebreath dissipates. Used Murmi is taken far away and dropped on a barren planet, and there, certain rites are performed to ensure that all potential for life is extinguished.

"From the very beginning I was fascinated by the Murmi and its inability to hold lifebreath for more than a short while," Borth was saying aloud to his accusers. "The creations I made of it became more and more beautiful and elaborate as I attempted to induce the clay to cling harder to the lifebreath I put into it, but in every case my creations ceased after a time to function.

"The more I thought of it, the more curious I became as to what this flaw would do to a life that bore it. How would an exquisite form react to the fading of lifebreath? How would it degenerate? How would it understand its degeneration? I wanted to try – to breath lifebreath into my Murmi creations. I spoke of this desire to the other students and my teachers. They were horrified and I was forbidden to think of it.

"I bided my time. I was a model student for a millenium or so, and only then did I dare volunteer to journey with a crew that disposed of Murmi. The load we had was unusable, of course, but I had some fresh Murmi in my pocket and in secret I spent many hours locked in my shiproom labouring over my creations. I made the most exquisite forms I had ever made, modelled on the Vaeri. Of course they were much tinier, for I had scant clay and nowhere to hide lifesized creatures. I did not bother with the wings, for they no longer served a purpose in my own kind. When I was finished, I wept to see how beautiful they were.

"I called my creatures Ur-lings."

In human words that would be translated as Little People, Borth sent to me.

"When we reached the place where the clay was to be thrown out, I pretended to be lost so that I could put my Ur-lings on the ground and breathe life into them. Then I left."

"Did you ever return?" one of the Vaeri asked.

Borth inclined his head, having picked up my habit of using body language to enhance speech or thoughts.

"Twice. I did not dare come again for fear I would be tracked. But the time I spent among the race arisen from my Ur-lings made me see the decadence and staleness of the Vaeri. The Ur-lings are neither smug nor complacent. Their lives contain pain and anger and sorrow, and they strive and yearn for beauty with every fibre of their beings. Life is infinitely more beautiful and precious, and even those who seek death, such as Awen-du, worship it as much as they fear it."

Of course, by now I knew that the name Borth had given me meant Forever, but only now did I understand why.

It was your radio and television emissions and satellite launches that attracted the attention of the Vaeri at last, Borth sent to me.

An expedition was sent and it was not difficult then to trace the source of the Murmi-based life forms back to Borth.

I am charged with creating monsters, he sent, coming the

full circle.

What will happen if they find you guilty? I thought.

I do not know. They will devise a punishment I suppose.

He did not look too worried. I suppose it is hard to worry about anything when you are an immortal.

"How can you have condemned these creatures to Murmi fate? Have you no guilt for the wrong you have done them?" asked a Vaeri. "Porsoul is mentally programmed for immortality. By using Murmi instead of perfect Porsoul you have condemned your creations to futility and despair. It is cruelty beyond imagining to make creatures into whose essence is woven the understanding of immortality, but to make them from a clay which will not hold lifebreath eternally."

I felt a stab of pure terror as I understood at last what the trial was about. A dozen different bits of information slid into place. Porsoul was immortal. Murmi was an imperfect form of Porsoul which, though it could capture the lifeforce breathed into it by its creator, could not continue to hold it. Borth had created humanity of Murmi.

In short, Borth Jesu H had given his precious creation mortality.

"This monster race cannot be allowed to go on," said another of the Vaeri, and I felt sick.

Borth spoke then, with greater eloquence than I had ever heard in his kind. So might a mother plead for the life of her baby.

"I do not care what punishment you bestow on me," he said at last. "But these creatures I have made deserve to live. Come with me and move among them. You will see then ..."

"I have seen how they live and what they make of the little lives you have bestowed on them, Borth Jesu H," said a grave, stern voice. "These Uman are greedy and violent. They rape their world and one another. They dwell in poverty and squalor, in hunger and despair. They live for instant gratification and exist in terror of death."

"But that is the thing," Borth said excitedly. "Don't you see? In spite of all that, they create, just as we do. They create beauty in their music and their words, in paintings and buildings and sculptures. They make for themselves a bittersweet immortality. Think of it! *No other race we have created, creates!"*

There was a long, strange silence at this.

Borth rushed on. "It is their fear of death, and their knowledge of its inevitability, that gives them such transcendent power. When Awen-du jumped from that bridge, she thought death was truth. She was prepared to give up her short and precious life to learn this single truth. Would any of us do such a thing? Would we have the courage or the greatness? These Ur-lings have a fleeting second – a minute lightness between birth and death which is their lives – yet they exist like a nova exploding in the infinite darkness of space. Our lives are dim candles beside theirs, for we have no passion, and our creations are as cold and perfect and lifeless as we ourselves have become. When we gave up death, we forgot to use our wings. We forgot to fly. In giving my Ur-lings mortality, I gave them passion and beauty. I gave them love and hate and desire. *I gave them wings."*

I began to laugh then, for I saw that this was the truth I had spent my life searching for. That broke up the proceedings because the Vaeri, who do not laugh, thought I was having some sort of fit.

The last time I saw Borth was as he waited for his sentence to be pronounced, for of course he had been found guilty.

They are going to send me to Earth, his thoughts floated into my mind.

Why? I thought fearfully, wondering if they would simply bomb the Earth and destroy both the creator and his creation.

No, Borth sent. *They cannot unmake. It is forbidden and has been since my people discovered immortality. They mean to expose me to the sun crystals which cause Porsoul to become Murmi.*

I did not understand and he was forced to say it more plainly.

I will be mortal there. They have elected to give me the gift of death. They have told me that I may move among my monsters and instruct them on the joys of death and mortality.

I was aghast for him, but he seemed unafraid.

I go uncaring. The Vaeri are a dead race – decadent and sterile. They became ghosts when they gave up death. If they saw your world and your people as I have, they would know that. Perhaps this is why they despise you so.

What will they do to me?

They will send you back as well. Borth hesitated. *They mean to offer you immortality and, through you, humanity. They have discovered a way to reverse the process of degeneration.*

We stared at one another for a time, as the other Vaeri began to assemble.

Good luck, I thought. Maybe I will see you on Earth.

I do not think so, Borth sent. *I wish you luck, Awen-du. And I hope immortality pleases you. But before you take what they offer, look upon the Vaeri and then upon your own race, and see who lives more sweetly.*

And his eyes asked a thing of me.

I returned to Earth. Borth was right: I did not see him again. I took the pills the Vaeri gave me, and these gave me immortality; not constant immortality, because I am made of Murmi, but a temporary immortality which could be extended infinitely by taking one pill after another. These pills prevent the degeneration from progressing. My life was immortal only by their grace, but the Vaeri told me that any offspring I had would be of unflawed Porsoul, so long as I was taking the pills at the moment of conception, and that these children would bear the seed of immortality.

Through me, humanity could grow to deathlessness.

I wanted to think, so I travelled. I grew no older outwardly, but inwardly I aged hundreds of years as I went about trying to see what part death played in our lives, and whether immortality would heal the ills of humanity.

In all that time, I let no man fertilise my ova and spawn a race of immortals. Whenever I saw something that made me consider it – a great man or woman dying, a great beauty fading – I thought of Borth's face, and the cold, dead eyes of the Vaeri.

Yet I could not resist it. I told myself I needed to live just a little longer to experience enough to ensure I made the right decision.

But the ages I lived began to weigh heavily, and with them came at last the truth of Borth's words, for with immortality had come deadness to my soul – a numbness and an emptiness. Worst of all, sometimes, when I looked into the mirror, Vaeri eyes stared out at me, and I was chilled.

So at last I did not take the pills, and now I grow old.

Oh I pray that I am mad enough and brave enough to do what I know Borth wanted, and that is to die. I am still afraid of it. Though I am old and creaky and withered, life is sweet to me, it has a beauty that brings me to tears. Sometimes it has such radiance that it fills my soul and pains me sweetly.

That is something the immortals can never know or feel.

Wait. Before you go, there is one last thing. It is my theory that laughter, which the Vaeri never understood, is the answer humanity has evolved to cope with the gift of Borth Jesu H. Thus my own much-maligned flippancy is an answer to the ultimate truths that I am privy to.

Borth? Well, I have often wondered what he found among his monsters. There had been talk of setting him back in time for some technical reason or other, and of course I cannot help but wonder if, by some strange chance, his is the body buried underneath the tower in the field next to the cemetery.

There is poetry in that thought.

If it was Borth buried under there, the only thing that nags at me is a desire to know why his arm was thrown out. Perhaps at the last irrevocable second, like any mortal, he feared death and flung up his arm to his brothers, the gods, in a futile plea for mercy.

Or maybe – and this is what I like to think – maybe, at that last minute, he felt the same great sweet sadness as I do to know he must lose his life and face the mystery of death, but his courage did not fail him. I picture him in my mind, lifting his arm and laughing as he gave his brothers the finger!

Oh yes. It pleases me to think our creator died laughing. I am, you see, an incurable romantic, and I like endings of all kinds to come with a flourish.

That is a very mortal thing to wish for. The Vaeri have no stories because they have no concept of endings – and stories must begin and end if they are to fly. But the Vaeri have forgotten how to use their wings. How dreary for them, poor things.

Afterword

Why do I write fantasy?

When I was young, I didn't much like the real world. Like so many kids who are misfits and loners, I spent a lot of time hiding out in the library. The books I loved most were not those that told stories of my own world, but those that told about worlds in which there were great heroes and courageous heroines, unicorns and magic; where animals could speak to you; where friends were loyal unto death, and love lasted forever; where truth and justice were not just words, and where one always fought for what one believed in: fantasy books.

They were never simply escape routes. They taught me about honour and beauty and courage and they made me yearn for more than just the material. They allowed me to return to my own world with renewed hope.

In part, I write fantasy for the same reasons as I read it – so that I can cast off this mortal coil – but also because there are issues I can confront better in parallel worlds than in my own. Fantasy is not easier to write than social realism. You must first be able to write well about the real world, then *you have to have the imagination to create a believable other world.*

Fantasy reflects and reaffirms our ideals. To my mind, no genre is more important in this grey and dissolute age.

The Blondefire Genome

Sean McMullen

Sean McMullen *is a computer analyst with the Bureau of Meteorology, and lives in Melbourne with his wife and daughter. He is a graduate of the University of Melbourne where he is still an instructor with the university karate club, and he has played and sung in several bands. He has had over two dozen SF stories published in Australia, Britain and the USA, and has twice won the Australian Ditmar Award for science fiction. His first book,* Call to the Edge, *was published in 1992, and his novel* Voices in the Light *in 1994.*

Megan walked home from school. She knew the bus would be full of kids talking about the Blondefire television special from the night before. Walking let her escape from hearing how well Jackie Cassall had danced and sung, and how great the local all-blonde girl group had been. Nobody had been watching the science program "Quantum". Not her science teacher, or her maths teacher, not a single student in the entire school. Megan had been on "Quantum".

Blondefire's latest hit was second on the Australian charts, ninth in Britain and fourteenth in the USA. They were going to make a series of video clips. The five girls who made up the group went to Megan's school, and everyone in the school was proud of them. Everyone except Megan.

Nobody who knew Megan had seen her appear on "Quantum" as for seven whole minutes she described her experiments with growing plants in a centrifuge at three times normal gravity. She had no tape of it. Her older brother, Alex, had cleared her timer setting on the family VCR to record the Blondefire special. Her mother had been on night shift at the medical laboratory and had missed the show. Her father was in England doing contract work.

Megan had told nobody beforehand: her television appearance was meant to be a surprise. Just as well, she thought.

They probably would have watched Blondefire anyway.

She arrived home and looked into her sunroom-greenhouse, staring at the spinning wheel of transparent plastic that induced three times the Earth's gravity for the plants inside.

"They don't even know you exist, but one day your seeds will fly into space," she told the plants. She walked upstairs to her attic laboratory and there, with the door locked behind her, she finally broke down and sobbed with frustration and disappointment.

Megan's interest in genetics had begun a year earlier, when her father had sent her a DNA kit for schools as a birthday present. She had used the reagents and instruments to extract DNA from the cells of plants, cut it up with enzymes, and then examined the pieces using electrophoresis. Soon she hit on the idea of growing wheat in a homemade centrifuge under high gravity and looking for genetic changes in each generation. With Alex's help, she had built a centrifuge: a tube of industrial plastic, fifteen centimetres in diameter, taped to a bicycle wheel rim and spun by an electric motor. It had spun almost continuously for months while several generations of wheat grew. Megan had painted the NASA logo on the outer rim. It was her ticket to space.

The DNA-ram, a version of the type invented at Cornell University in 1983, was all her own work. A starter's pistol was clamped into one of two tubes welded into an old pressure cooker, and a hand-operated vacuum pump was connected to the other tube. When the pistol fired its blank, the blast was diverted into a pressure tube to shoot a hollow plastic cylinder down another tube until it hit a plate with a tiny hole at the centre. A mixture of powdered tungsten and DNA sprayed through the hole and into the evacuated pressure cooker, which contained a dish of ryegrass stem cells. It was a rough, random process, but some of the DNA on the tungsten particles was rammed into the cells, and their genetic makeup was altered forever.

Experimental work helped to ease Megan's pain at the way her appearance on national television the night before had been ignored. She had extracted DNA from wattle leaves some days earlier using an ethanol precipitation method, and now she mixed the raw DNA with a pinch of tungsten powder. Preparing the target ryegrass stem cells took time, as did pumping air out of the pressure cooker with the hand pump.

Three hours passed as if they had been moments. Megan heard Alex come in and immediately start playing the video of the Blondefire special. She raised her hands to her ears, then forced them down again. She loaded a blank cartridge into the starter's pistol.

"This is for you, Blondefire," she said as she squeezed the trigger.

A muffled thud rammed the tungsten and DNA mixture into the target cells. Megan broke the seal on the pressure cooker and lifted out the dish of cells. The tissue culture process to make the enhanced cells of ryegrass was a difficult one, and it would keep her mind off Blondefire for the evening.

When she went downstairs to microwave a pizza for dinner Alex was still watching Blondefire. Jackie Cassall was all legs, lycra and billowing, bushy hair, singing "Saturday to Sunday" and looking wholesome, winsome and dynamic. Her face was wonderfully clear and smooth, while Megan was conscious that her own was ravaged by acne. She looked down at the pizza that she was carrying and imagined her face in the disk.

"I'm fifteen, acne happens around fifteen," she muttered to herself.

"Sorry, what was that?" asked Alex.

"Ah, Jackie Cassall's skin. I just can't believe skin as good as that," she replied.

"Yeah, she's great. Hey, sorry about not recording 'Quantum' last night. What was on, did you ring the studio?"

"Just a live show, some kids with their science projects," Megan replied coldly.

She took the pizza to her bedroom and lay on her bed, eating the slices and examining her face in a mirror. Her skin was seldom without a spot or two, but something had brought on a particularly bad case of acne six weeks ago. What had caused the zits? Some new food? Her flu shots? Her diary might have a clue.

She leafed through the pages, looking over her plant experiment notes and personal entries. She was fanatically careful about experimental records and she had documented her acne right down to an entry for each pimple. She booted up her mother's PC and ran Statistica, then entered her acne count for each day over three months.

"A base rate of two or three zits per week. Annoying, but not the end of the world," she told the figures on the screen. The count had risen abruptly to fifteen per week, then peaked at twenty-one before trailing down to the present seven.

The rise was sharp, so it had to be something new and obvious: food, perhaps, or makeup? Some manufacturer might have changed an ingredient, added something that had caused an allergy. Laboratory chemicals were another suspect. Her experiments involved some exotic compounds, and she had documented those in the diary, too.

She typed in the figures on when she had begun using different chemicals, along with what she could piece together on food and makeup. On the screen the lines of the graphs remained stubbornly smooth and consistent near the date where her acne had suddenly erupted. There was nothing else in her diary but a note about the pollination of ryegrass variety CG-47.

Megan sat back and closed her eyes. Pollen! Ryegrass pollen induced hay fever and allergies in some people, but *this* ryegrass had been genetically hacked with wattle DNA. Could it unbalance oil levels in her skin? Ryegrass pollen that caused zits. Zitgrass. But the makeshift greenhouse was in the sunroom, so why weren't her mother and Alex affected? Perhaps it was related to teenage hormone levels. Alex was twenty, her mother forty-five.

Almost as if he had been given a telepathic cue, Alex turned up the television's sound. "And now Blondefire's first big hit, 'Blondefire, My Desire'," cried the compere.

Something inside Megan slipped free from its chain. An image of creamy white skin spotted with angry red eruptions appeared in her mind. Hardly aware of what she was doing, she opened her battered filing cabinet full of seed envelopes. She retrieved the envelope marked RYE/WATTLE CG-47 and poured a few seeds into her palm. Blondefire sang on from the living-room. Megan stared at her genetic creations, then went to the sunroom-greenhouse.

"Blondefire made me vanish. I might as well never have been on 'Quantum'," she told the seeds as she sprinkled them into a tray of seedling mix. "Now I'll make Blondefire vanish."

Under artificial lighting and heating, the seeds sprouted and the seedlings flourished. Megan collected every seed from the mature plants, avoiding contact with the pollen by breathing through a long tube running outside the greenhouse. By the time several generations of plants had passed, she had thousands of seeds.

Spring came. The ryegrass that sprouted in gardens and

vacant blocks near where the Blondefire singers lived was quite normal to look at, but the local chemists noticed a sudden increase in demand for acne creams and lotions from teenagers. With forced detachment Megan observed the thick, carefully applied makeup that now started to appear on Jackie Cassall's face.

One morning there was anxious talk around the school. Jackie was leaving Blondefire. Jackie had zits. Jackie had been asked to go. The lead singer took it bravely, and said that it was not all bad, because now she would be free to study for her exams.

Another member of the group, Josie Allen, was next. She had been saved from the first sowing of zitgrass by the industrious gardeners who lived in her street, but Megan had also scattered seeds in a vacant lot beside her bus stop, and these seeds had sprouted more slowly in the less fertile soil there.

Soon there was another Blondefire scandal as Josie was ejected. She did not go quietly. The manager wanted her to retire and concentrate on writing lyrics for Blondefire songs, but Josie refused. It was full performer status or nothing. All the remaining girls were true albinos rather than just being naturally blonde, and there was something in the biochemistry of their skin that made them immune to the zitgrass pollen. When Josie's parents threatened to sue over the use of the Blondefire name they re-formed as Whitefire, but with the lead singer, songwriter and name gone, the group struggled on for only a few months before disbanding. Megan was surprised by the speed with which Jackie and Josie had been dumped, but it confirmed her suspicions about personal loyalties in show business.

The plague of acne struck dozens of others in the school, always those between twelve and seventeen. Megan noticed that although Jackie's face was a mess, she remained as sociable as ever while taking far more interest in schoolwork. Years of balancing study against Blondefire commitments had left her with average grades, but within two months of the zit plague she was getting A for everything.

Is there anything she can't do? Megan wondered nervously. Now there was another contender for the title of school genius. She stared at a poster of the space shuttle on the classroom wall. It was captioned "To Jackie, from your fans in space", and was signed by three astronauts.

I taught you about shallow friends, Megan thought, and she refused to feel guilty.

Megan's final year at school began badly. Her father ran out of contract work in England, and could send no money home. The strain of paying Megan's school fees meant that her mother had little money to spare for her daughter's experiments. Megan suspended most of her work and decided that she would "discover" zitgrass growing wild once she was at university, and had access to proper laboratories. Her centrifuge spun on, however, the excess electricity draining most of her allowance. It was her ticket to space, it was everything. When she got to university she would meet scientists who knew people at NASA. They would help to get her 3g seeds onto the space shuttle.

For Megan, the school year could not end too quickly. Jackie's grades continued to improve, and Megan often noticed that Jackie and her circle of friends were watching her. She became withdrawn, because she found it difficult to make small talk with classmates who were obviously talking about her behind her back. Jackie handled assignments and assessment tasks as easily as a letter of thanks for a birthday present.

Finally the ultimate nightmare happened: Jackie scored an A++ in a minor physics assignment, while Megan could manage only A+. Megan had not come second to anyone in a science subject in five years.

Once more Megan shunned the bus and walked home. "Now I know what she's been saying," she told herself. "She's been saying I'm not as good as everyone thought, that she's better. Well, stuff them all, I only study for myself! I don't care what her results are!"

She resolved not even to check the results of her assignments from now on. Soon she would be at university, free of jealous classmates whispering behind her back, free of the huge blue eyes that stared at her out of Jackie's scarred and mottled face. She checked the plants in her centrifuge, then booted up her mother's PC and accessed a file. It was the proposal to NASA, which she had been crafting for months: how would the seeds of plants grown for several generations at 3g grow in weightless conditions? It would be such a simple experiment to fly on a space shuttle.

Alex's voice echoed from the living-room.

"Hey Meg, come and watch this!"

"I'm studying, Lex."

"Stuff the study. You'll want to see this."

"... great discovery!" The words caught her attention as she approached the living-room. Alex was watching "Rockin' and Ravin'", a live studio show.

"This is a pop music show for kids," Megan objected.

"Just listen, it'll blow you away."

"And now for something way, way different that you just won't believe," bawled Danny Donohue, the compere.

"Who is this flatliner?" sneered Megan.

"Shush, just listen."

"Remember Jackie Cassall? Well, after she split with Blondefire she got into science! And whaddaya think happened? Schoolgirl scientist Jackie Cassall has discovered a type of ryegrass that causes zits! Here she is now to tell us about zitgrass – "

Megan gasped so hard that she had a coughing fit. *Her* discovery – and *her name* for it as well! By the time she had her breath back under control Jackie was speaking.

"I got a really bad case of zits last spring, bad like you wouldn't believe. I had to leave Blondefire, I couldn't go on camera with a face like the surface of the moon. I decided to work out just why I'd suddenly got so many zits, so I began to study up on science a lot more."

"How long did it take to spot the cause?"

"Months. I doorknocked every house in the neighbourhood and asked the kids to tell me if they'd had a bad case of zits lately. I did a scatter map of what I found, and sure enough there were hot spots. I lived right at the centre of one. That made me think that it might be caused by something in the air, a chemical or something. I checked with the Environmental Protection Agency on chemical spills, but no luck. Then I wondered if some rare plant had become trendy with the local gardeners, so I doorknocked again. Eventually I narrowed the cause down to ryegrass."

Jackie had discovered zitgrass growing wild! Although she was gearing her language to a pop music audience, it was obvious that there was a sharp mind behind the words. She said that university scientists had agreed to let her use their laboratory free.

Megan closed her eyes, but forced herself to stay and listen.

"So, airhead to egghead in one year?" said the compere, with a wink for the camera.

"Oh no, I've always liked science. When the zits got me I realised that as a member of Blondefire I had nothing more than a great face and voice, and now the face was gone. So, I began studying really hard."

The compere smiled smugly. "Hey, but who cares if a few kids in a rich country have zits? Why didn't you work on ways to feed the kids in Africa?"

Jackie took an inhaler from her coat pocket. "See this? It looks like an asthma inhaler, but I charged it with zitgrass pollen before coming here," she said to the compere. Then she faced the audience. "He says zits are okay!" she shouted.

The audience hissed loudly in reply.

"Brace yourself, Danny, here come the zits!" Jackie walked towards the compere, who panicked and ran. She chased him to the edge of the stage with the inhaler. He blundered into some props and went sprawling, then scrambled out of sight.

The teenage audience cheered and hooted its approval as Jackie swaggered back to centre stage.

She tossed the inhaler in the air and caught it. "Actually this really is only an asthma inhaler, it's safe. I gave myself asthma sniffing hundreds of types of pollen for six months. Danny might think smart kids are nerds, but where his precious skin is concerned, he listens to what nerds say."

"She's a knockout!" said Alex.

"Shuddup!" snapped Megan.

"Everyone out there, but especially you Melbourne kids between ten and twenty kilometres south of the Yarra, get out there and rip out the ryegrass next spring. Send samples in to the CSIRO so we can work out just how far this new type of zitgrass has spread. And remember: scientists have all the fun – "

A commercial cut her short.

"So *that's* why she chose a pop music show on prime time," Megan said. "She's recruiting a huge team of free research assistants."

"Wasn't she great, wasn't she just great?" babbled Alex. "D'you know her from school? Could you tell her you have this real spunk of a brother who's into science?"

"I could, Lex, but I'd be lying."

The commercials ended, and "Rockin' and Ravin'" went straight into a video clip. Megan shambled off to her room. A year ago she had crushed Blondefire like a beetle underfoot, but now she lurked in the shadows, defeated, while Jackie was a triumphant hero.

She sat on the edge of her bed. Jackie Cassall, teenage scientist. I made her what she is, she thought. I created her. She's already ahead of me. How long before she realises that gene hacking created zitgrass? I'm the first one she would check in the hunt for a gene hacker. What I did probably breaches the Geneva Convention on Germ Warfare.

Megan shuddered, then stood up. She had not allowed herself to think of the consequences when she had been preparing the zitgrass plague. Jackie had to be stopped before she learned the truth, if it wasn't already too late. She went to the attic and took her DNA-ram apart, then returned downstairs with the starter's pistol.

"I have to go out for a while, Lex. Can I borrow your bike and your helmet?"

"No problem."

"Before I forget, here's your starter's pistol back."

"What? Oh, that. Are you sure?"

"I'm sure."

"What about your experiment?"

"It's finished. It was ... disappointing."

Megan packed maps, diagrams, chromatograph charts and seeds into a large envelope, then scribbled a note.

Jackie, this enclosed info may help you. I created zitgrass in an amateur genetic engineering experiment. I must have had pollen and seeds on my clothing, and spread them when I went jogging. When the zit plague started I panicked and tried to cover up. I am truly sorry for what happened to you and everyone else, and I accept full blame. Congrats on your scientific investigation, it was brilliant.

Megan Warnall

She hated to accuse herself of incompetence, but that was better than confessing the truth and risking a jail term for bio-terrorism. There was still one last reparation to be made: dizzy with anguish, she printed out the draft of her letter to NASA about the 3g seeds.

When she reached Jackie's place the lights were on. Good: her parents were there to take the package. She couldn't be back from the studio yet.

But Jackie answered the doorbell.

"Megan!" she exclaimed.

"I didn't expect you to be home. The – ah, television show."

"You mean 'Rockin' and Ravin'?" laughed Jackie. "Danny locked himself in a toilet and refused to come out while I was still there. The studio hands bundled me into a taxi while the commercials were on and had me driven home."

Megan clutched the envelope and stared down at the doormat. This was not the way she had wanted it.

"These are maps of zitgrass distribution that I've compiled," she said, thrusting the envelope into Jackie's hands.

"Zitgrass!" Jackie exclaimed. She looked inside. "You – but there's so much in here."

"It might make your work easier. There's chromatograph data and other stuff that might help too, and – I'd better go."

"No, wait," cried Jackie, following Megan down the path. "How long have you known about zitgrass?"

"Ten months."

"Ten – so you discovered it first!"

"But you published first."

"'Rockin' and Ravin'' is hardly publication."

Megan took a deep breath and reached into the envelope. "This note explains everything. Read it."

"We'll have to – "

"Read it! Please!" Megan could not stop the tears of humiliation that ran down her cheeks. "I've been a prize idiot and a coward too, Jackie. What can I say? Sorry I trashed your career?"

Jackie finished reading the note and looked up, eyes wide and unblinking. "This is unreal," she said. "You hacked a genome, you created a new species. That's fantastic."

"It's also morally indefensible," Megan said miserably. That's odd, she thought. She hasn't done a total meltdown yet. She seems to admire me for creating what ruined her face.

"What is in this note would confirm some people's worst fears about science," Jackie said slowly. "Loud, stupid people like Danny Donohue." She put a hand on Megan's shoulder. "Besides, why punish you for an accident? Let's burn the note and forget what you did."

I don't believe this, thought Megan. How could anyone forgive as easily as that? "I should have concentrated on my 3g plants," she mumbled.

"Yes, I know about your centrifuge. I saw you on 'Quantum' last year, it was unreal – "

"What!" Megan dropped Alex's helmet in surprise. "How –

I mean, it clashed with the Blondefire show."

"I set the timer on my VCR. I never miss 'Quantum'."

"I thought nobody from school had seen it. My brain-dead brother reset our VCR to record the Blondefire special, so I never saw the show either."

"Come inside," said Jackie. "I'll play you the tape. I've already shown it to my friends at school. Do you drink coffee?"

Megan did not, but she accepted a mug of milk coffee anyway. So *that's* what the whispering at school was about, she realised. They actually admired her!

"When you ... broke up with Blondefire I was, well, so sorry for you, and it was all my fault."

Jackie shook her head and grinned ruefully. "Show business is cruel and crazy. Image is everything. I couldn't have a boyfriend because some fans might get jealous. I couldn't get high grades because some fans might be intimidated."

"Then why stay with it?"

"When you're very good at something it's hard to stop, even if you really don't give a stuff. Don't get me wrong, though. When the zits hit me, I cried for days. Then my father pointed out that while my IQ score was at the top of the measurable range, my grades were only so-so. I took the point and threw everything into my study. Hey, don't look so guilty. I'm happy now."

Not good enough, Megan thought. I deliberately hurt her, then I lied about it, and now I get off the hook for free. Not good enough, Megan Warnall.

"Jackie, what are you working on now besides zitgrass?"

"Just study. I want to get into university."

"You have fans at NASA, don't you?"

"That's right. They're nice people."

Two years of work! a horrified voice screamed inside Megan.

The greatest achievement of your life! She has no right to share it! This project is yours, all yours!

Megan took out her letter to NASA.

"Get on to your NASA contacts, send them this proposal for a space shuttle project. It's to fly seeds from my plants grown in 3g for two years. Tell them you want to see how they grow when weightless. They'll buy it for sure."

"Take your work? I couldn't – "

"Yes you could. You can handle publicity, I can't."

"I'd rather just be friends with you, I don't want to rob your work."

"No Jackie – look, you recruited a team tonight to fight zitgrass. Team up with me as well. Both of our names will go into space with those seeds. I'm not just trying to make up for killing Blondefire, I really need you."

"But I haven't even seen your laboratory, and I've got another media interview tomorrow."

"Well, come back to my place now."

"What about the 'Quantum' video?"

"Bring it with you."

Alex was asleep in front of a replay of *Terminator* 2 when Megan got home. She dropped his helmet beside him.

"Wake up Lex, I've made a great scientific discovery."

"So zitgrass is a Martian plot?" he yawned.

Close, thought Megan. "No, I've learned that science only works as a team effort."

"Whoopee-do."

"I'm forming a team to get my 3g seeds into space. Interested?"

"What's in it for me?"

"Jackie Cassall is my other recruit. She's outside, chaining up her bike – "

Alex gasped and sprang up, knocking his chair over as he scrambled out to the bathroom and turned on the shower. Megan smirked as she straightened the chair.

Jackie came in, holding the "Quantum" video cassette.

"The greenhouse and centrifuge are through this door," said Megan, taking out a key. "The rest is upstairs."

"What about this?" asked Jackie, holding up the cassette.

Megan shrugged. Somehow her first television appearance had become something unimportant from the distant past. "It can wait," she said as she unlocked the door. "Let's look at the real thing first."

Afterword

I write SF for several reasons. One is that I just enjoy writing, and watching characters come alive. Another is the same reason that I work in a scientific organisation: I like taking ideas and developing them into something bigger and more interesting. Yet another reason is that SF can be used to model possible futures (just as computers model the weather) to see what can go wrong. "The Blondefire Genome" is in the latter category. With all the media fuss about computer hacking in recent years, it surprises me that nobody has paid much attention to the potential problem of genetic hacking. It is a little harder than computer hacking, but is well within the reach of any bright high school student. Not only are all the gene hacking techniques described in this story real, they are about ten years old.

"The Blondefire Genome" is also an attack on the popular stereotype of scientists. Most are not introverted losers: they are friendly, dynamic people who are good at working in teams. Even if not many of them can sing well, and a few are not much to look at, they are often as bright and as multi-talented as Jackie.

Everything

Mustafa Zabirovic

Mustafa Zahirovic *is twenty-four years old, lives in Melbourne, and is a physiotherapist. He says: "Over the past couple of years I have been treating my writing more seriously and my first professional sale now appears on the inside of a tram somewhere. I have yet to see it, but apparently it's read by commuters daily.*

"As well as short stories I enjoy writing poetry and film scripts. I hope to explore all these interests further and to complete a novel in the near future. I am encouraged by the success of my shorter fiction, which has been printed in both professional and small-press magazines in Australia and overseas."

People keep screaming about the wisdom of hindsight. About standing back from a situation to get an objective view. They have no idea how easy that can be with the aid of technology. Surgical exchange. New eyes gave me a new look at life.

For a time I thought I could have been a painter. But there's something different about the colours now. Through my new eyes they seem duller, flatter. I still enjoy looking, but everything seems older.

I don't think about painting any more. My memories don't take form in colours and shapes, they take form in words. At least I'm still able to write things down, I wasn't cheated out of that. Technology, everything!

Before the change, my life revolved around just three things, the only things I ever enjoyed doing. Going to the steelworks or to Ivan's studio, or watching the rain. My triad. All simple and satisfying. Reaching out and gathering my life together.

It was at the steelworks that I first became aware of the change. I had spent half of the school day and part of the evening quietly watching the workers from between the scrap metal bins. I was about to leave when, suddenly and quite unreasonably, reality disappeared. In its place stood a flock of burning sheep. It was the first image that came into my mind.

All along the process lines, the hot metal slabs coming out of the presses glowed brightly white. The light was so intense, I had to turn away. But everything else in the factory looked normal. When I glanced back at the presses my sheep were again just hot slabs of metal. "Work of the artist's mind," as Ivan would say.

It was strange, I had to admit. But readily forgettable. I wasn't even sure that it had happened at all. And even if it had, I thought at the time, did it really matter?

It was quite dark by the time I left for Ivan's studio. There was a lovely misty rain all around, so I didn't rush. I knew I wouldn't get really wet. Fat drops of water formed on my eyelashes, and in the beam of streetlights made stars when I blinked. Then between these stars there was other light, strangely out of place. And I knew it was the change again.

The car exhaust pipes everywhere looked glaringly bright. Even the exhaust was glowing. It was like steam rising off hot water, bright exhaust rising up from the street. I walked through the exhaust trail of cars stopped at the lights and kicked at the glowing fumes. Alone, the change would have made a normal street scene look strangely attractive, but blended with the misty rain it was perfect.

After a time I found that if I concentrated, I could turn the effect off and on. I could have it either way – plain and boring or with a touch of brilliance. I felt comfortable with the change. Like I could control it, like it was mine.

I was blissfully unaware of any possible harmful outcomes. Neither did it occur to me that the change might be permanent. While simple curiosity consumed me, the arms of my triad were being broken.

At the studio Ivan was cooking. He looked up as I walked

in. "Hard day of school, Niklaus?"

"I didn't go."

"Why are you never in school?"

"This is why." I put a few pieces of scrap metal on his workbench. He often used them in his sculptures.

"You miss on school to go to the steel factory?"

I didn't answer.

He half frowned, half smiled. "The steel factory makes four tonnes of waste in a day and *this* is all you bring?"

"Da, this is all I bring."

Ivan smiled. He liked it when I made fun of his Polish accent.

"So. You would like to eat?"

"Is it chicken soup again?"

"Of course."

"I'm not hungry."

Ivan went off into a mumble, something like thinking out loud but done with lots of hand gestures. "You don't go into school, you don't eat, you don't do many things, but all day you could spend in the rain."

I settled down on his couch.

"And you sleep on my couch! You must be a humble sleeper. If you can sleep on this couch you could sleep absolutely anywhere, definitely, you could sleep even on the rocks."

Ivan's mumbling continued as he went to work on another painting. Finally I fell asleep to the sounds of his voice and the rain growing heavy on the roof.

Now you can hear *me* scream about the wisdom of hindsight. I can't paint it but I can write it. In some ways it's better. What colour would I paint my lack of action?

I knew something strange was happening to me, but I was content to do nothing. It was like looking at the rain – there was something pleasant and relaxing about just watching. But in my sleep I must have been concentrating on it. In between dreams the change suddenly made sense and the realisation woke me. I lay awake thinking about it till the morning. The answer seemed so obvious.

That morning I watched carefully as Ivan had his breakfast. His bowl of soup went from a bright white light to a hazy yellow glow as the liquid cooled. His lips glowed for a few seconds every time he took another mouthful. Wisps of light crept up from his spoon as he sat it on the edge of his easel. I felt like I was getting used to the change. My sensitivity was getting finer.

Ivan saw the way I was staring at him. He gave me one of his strange looks; the one where he lifts one eyebrow and tilts his head.

"What is the feeling with you this morning?"

"What?"

"Didn't you sleep well?"

"Oh ... You mean, 'How am I feeling? What's the *matter* with me this morning?'"

"Yes. Yes of course. My brain for English does not work well in the mornings."

"I'm fine."

"You do not look fine."

"I'm okay."

"If something was wrong of course you would tell me. True?"

I smiled. "I'd even make up something if it would stop all these questions."

He snorted with feigned grumpiness. "Everything!" And with that he ended the conversation.

"Everything" was an expression Ivan used on occasion, and I liked it. When said with a level of amazement and sarcasm it meant "Now I've seen everything!". But when *I* used it, the meaning was in my tone of voice. Ivan grew to understand it after a while.

As it happened I didn't go to school that day. I'm sure no one noticed or cared. Instead I spent the day riding the trains into and out of the suburbs. I let the change sweep over me without controlling it at all. I liked watching the brightness and dullness. I liked watching the rain wash the glow out of objects as they cooled.

With some practice I could even pick up light coming off people's faces. At first I could see it only on people who had run to catch the train. Their warm, flushed cheeks were very bright. But later it was visible on everyone. Columns of brightness rose from their faces and hands, and gently mingled to form waves of light. I felt like I was immersed in a current of radiance. A current that surrounded all these people and joined them, like they were part of something odd and beautiful.

Even if it was only an illusion, I didn't want it to stop. But despite my efforts, reality was impossible to avoid once I got home. As Ivan would say, "The walls are shaking." Dad made sure of that.

He was perpetually in a bad mood. If one thing didn't start him boiling it was another: work all day and still can't meet the bills; woman doesn't pay me respect; that damn boy is never home. Whatever the reason was today, Dad was bristling. He was pacing up and down in the lounge and I watched him quietly from the shadows in the hallway. He had one fist clenched, the other on a bottle of tequila. That was his favourite combination.

Mum sat quietly, careful to keep her eyes low. She had nothing more than a pale glow radiating from her. The glow was flat and weak, like her spirit. It was slightly brighter around one eye. I could see it was bruised.

While Mum was only a glow, Dad was like a mushrooming explosion. He was ringed with energy and light. He had stripped down to the waist and there was bright white steam rising from his back. He was like a fiery ball of malice.

Dad saw me moving in the shadows of the hallway. I backed away quietly to my bedroom, but there was no point. I knew he'd follow me. In the darkness his face and chest were seething with light. He was shouting something but I couldn't make out the words. I was too scared.

I wasn't afraid that Dad would hit me. I knew he would. I was scared because I couldn't turn off the effects of the change. I really needed to see everything normally, and I couldn't.

Dad slammed a glowing hand across my face. Then he drank from his bottle, yelled something and walked out. I left glowing droplets of blood on the floor and on the bedsheets.

Quite suddenly I felt paranoid and intensely afraid. I felt like I couldn't get out. Like I was trapped inside the change. That things would never return to normal.

I didn't know what to do. I was afraid to open my eyes, afraid to close them.

I remember how unsteady I was as I walked around my bed. My legs quivered as if they didn't belong to me. I brushed my hand against the wall and left behind a glowing handprint. There was a time when I would have found this new trick interesting, but that night it terrified me.

I curled up on the floor. All my senses were spread out to different corners of the room. Awareness of one sense automatically took another away from me. If I could hear, I was blind. If I could see, I couldn't feel.

But one thing was always there. The terrible darkness. Not dream, not nightmare, just the black emptiness of being totally alone. And the whole time just one thought, "Will I ever be normal?"

Then there was sleep.

The next morning the house was cold and lifeless. Both Mum and Dad had gone to work.

I walked aimlessly in and out of rooms. I seemed whole again. My head and tongue felt tired and my knees ached from sleeping on the floor, but I was united, and grateful.

Numbly I watched my glowing footprints fade away. I was almost too exhausted for emotion. The rooms were filled with signs of the change. The hazy yellow pulse coming from the television. The humming glow seeping out from behind the fridge.

I wanted Ivan to be at home with me then, and I felt embarrassed by the idea. Not because I needed someone to be with, especially that morning, but because Ivan had never seen where or how I lived. And I guess I wanted to keep it that way.

I finished my idle wandering in the kitchen. The sight of my parents' breakfast dishes reminded me of how long it had been since I last ate.

I went to the fridge and opened the door. The wave of black air that poured out over the floor was so unexpected that I jumped back. I stared at the macabre black pit in the fridge. By the time the cold air hit my ankles I was well into a flashback to the night before. I was aware only of the blackness – the loneliness. Isolation. I couldn't change anything. I would never be normal again.

My exhausted emotions were quickly replaced by the energy of fear. I slammed the fridge door shut and backed away. There were still curly wisps of cold black air on the floor as I turned and started to run.

I can't remember how I got to Ivan's place, or how long it

took, or how I sliced some skin off my heel. But I *can* remember how I felt. Like I was being punished. That all this was somehow my fault, that I deserved it.

Ivan was working with the blowtorch. Heating metal and then bending it. He turned towards me as I rushed in the door of his studio. The brightness of the flame stunned me. I must have screamed a little.

Ivan came running to help.

"Niklaus. What is it?"

"My eyes."

"What happened? Your foot is bleeding."

"I don't know what to do."

"Tell me what did you do? I can't see what it is."

"My eyes, my eyes."

"What is wrong?"

"The change."

"I am not understanding you."

But his actions understood. He took a tea-towel and wrapped it around my head, covering my eyes. It helped me calm down. It was dark but not lonely, just relaxing.

That's how I was to spend the next few days. Living on Ivan's couch with a dishcloth wrapped around my head. I slept easily, and ate all of Ivan's variations of chicken soup. For a short time the stinging in my heel, where the skin had been sliced away, was the only reminder of what had happened at home.

I knew that at Ivan's studio I was safe, like always. I didn't feel I had to go anywhere, definitely not home, not anywhere. And that was good. All I had to do was tell the story of the change. First to Ivan, then to other people.

Yosman was the first person after Ivan to hear my story. I'd met him only once before at the studio and remembered him as being abrupt and pushy. Ivan didn't really like him but tolerated his occasional visits when he tried to sell his "wares" or offer shady investment deals. He had come by to do just that, and I must have caught his attention sitting blindfolded on the couch.

"Listen to Niklaus' story," Ivan told him. "I am needing help to understand it."

I told Yosman about the steelworks and then about the car exhaust, but he seemed impatient. He kept uh-humming and ah-hahing. As the story progressed he became quieter. Until he just stood there, very close to me. I could hear him breathing.

"Yosman. What do you say?" Ivan asked from across the room.

"Not now, Ivan. I'm thinking."

There were a few minutes of silence. I heard Yosman walk past me. He started making slow circles around the couch where I sat, clunking his boot heels firmly on the concrete floor.

"Yosman. Perhaps the boy should be seen by a doctor."

Again there was a short silence, then, "No. Absolutely not. Nobody leaves until I get back." I heard him go clunking out the door. Not quite running.

Much later that night there were voices as I slept. I heard them fade in slowly.

"Why are you like this? Look at how young he is."

"You've got no idea how much the little bastard is worth."

"I'm thinking to seek proper medical attention for Niklaus."

"Like the military don't have doctors."

"You don't understand these people. They are like vultures."

"Give me vultures with unlimited funding any time. Wake up. Do you wanna live in this hole forever?"

"I cannot believe …"

The voices faded into a slur of sound, narrowly missing my consciousness. Then they returned.

"... and believe me when I am saying there are people I can tell all about this."

"These gentlemen I know won't want this made public."

"That is exactly what I will be doing."

"Just how healthy do you want to stay?"

"Pah! You cannot threaten me. Listen, when – "

"No. Now *you* listen up ..."

The words became lost in the static of half sleep as the slur of sound continued.

For the next three days more people came to Ivan's studio. I wore my blindfold the whole time, but even before they were introduced to me I knew that I had never met them. Ivan was very quiet. He just showed them in and showed them out again. I had the feeling he didn't know them either.

The first stranger woke me from my sleep to ask me questions. As I repeated my story Yosman stood by and added details, sounding very excited. Very keen to please. That said a lot.

Yosman struck me as being a small-time hood, a petty opportunist. However he chose to measure it, these people must have been more powerful than he was, or he wouldn't have been so polite. I had no reason to believe they were any more legitimate than Yosman. What sort of honest businessman visits in the middle of the night?

The second evening another one came. He was loud and cocky, and shot questions at me quickly. Yosman and the first stranger stood around being polite. The whole thing was falling into a pattern.

By the third night I knew what to expect, I didn't even try to go to sleep. Yosman and the first two strangers were there, but they didn't talk to me or ask me questions. I was surprised by how quiet they were. They were waiting nervously, and it made the whole studio seem tense. I felt as if everything was about to be resolved.

Ivan sat down next to me on the couch. "Niklaus, how are you feeling?"

"A bit worried."

"Mmm. On this I understand you."

"What's going to happen, Ivan?"

"I am thinking that I am more in the darkness than you with your blindfold."

There was a short silence, then I heard Ivan chuckle quietly.

"What?" I asked.

"This whole scene carries much of the symbolism, do you see it?"

"Obviously not," I said, pointing to the blindfold.

"Imagine this, Niklaus. You are the child Christ in the manger to be visited upon by the three men of wisdom. You see, these strangers are like the wise men. Two are here already, and tonight must be the third wise stranger to come."

"Great." I wasn't too impressed.

"But of the nativity scene this is the opposite completely. Not three wise men, but three sly men."

"And what about Yosman?"

"He is the donkey in the background."

True, that *was* worth a chuckle. But the tension of the situation couldn't be denied. I asked Ivan, "But do these three men bear gifts, or take them away?"

There was a knock at the door before he could answer my question. He got up, but added quickly, "Be careful, Niklaus."

I sat alone on the couch and listened to firm, steady footsteps coming towards me from the door. With them came the smell of clean paper and wine.

"How do you do, young man?"

"Okay."

"Do you know who I am?"

"No."

"My name is Gerard Simon." I sat quietly. "It sounds like very little has been explained to you about how I can help."

"No one's told me anything." I imagined Gerard Simon looking around the studio at his accomplices. Yosman and the first two strangers were silent. "How *can* you help?"

"Now is not the time. I believe in due course we can – "

"How?"

A few murmurs circulated among the accomplices. Low, deep sounds. Like they were sounding their disapproval at my question.

"Well, I'm not sure you'll understand."

"Give the boy a chance." Ivan's voice was resolute.

"Of course." Gerard Simon paused. It felt like he was trying to stare Ivan down. "I deal in information. Quite simple. I am the meeting point between a supply and a demand. If something useful arises, however obscure, I need to know because my clients need to know. Presently, certain clients are very interested in your situation, young man. You understand so far?"

I nodded.

"Good. And I'm sure you'll appreciate that these parties would like to maintain a level of secrecy."

"Mainly because this is illegal, military or not." Ivan would not be quietened, and again there were murmurs. I had the feeling Ivan was on the right track. This Gerard Simon reminded me of Yosman. He was just an opportunist on a much bigger scale.

Gerard Simon continued, "We can have your eyes transplanted – "

"What is the failure chances?" Ivan stood closer to me now.

"Shut up, Ivan." Yosman spoke his first words that night.

"We can successfully transplant your eyes, that's how advanced the surgery is. We can help you see normally again."

"Niklaus, be careful." Ivan's voice had a feeling of urgency. "You do not have to decide anything now."

"Ivan!" Yosman's shrill pitch echoed in the studio for a second.

There was some sort of shuffling and then a heavy sound. A gasp. And other footsteps all around.

"Damn you into hell, Yosman. The world will know of what is happening here today."

"There are people I can talk to about you too."

"There is no such thing as a threat."

"Believe me now. Just shut up."

"I will not."

"Ivan the martyr. Oh, you're making me cry."

"Enough of the circus." Gerard Simon's voice was cold. He swept up all the room's energy into his words, and there was nothing to do other than be still and listen.

He cleared his throat. "I'm offering to help you see normally again. We're not here to hurt you. Only to help. Do you want me to make things better?"

Make things better. It was like he was talking to a five-year-old. It would be easy to slip into this quick and comfortable solution. I felt myself sliding in. I couldn't help it. *Make things better. Make things better.* It kept rolling in my head.

"You can see it is the boy needs time."

"It's okay, Ivan. I want them to help me."

"Good. We'll talk more at the clinic." Gerard Simon's voice had changed. It seemed a little more aggressive.

"Come with me, Ivan."

"No." Gerard Simon and Yosman spoke in unison.

Gerard Simon continued, "If we want the best results we can't delay. No one to hold your hand. No change of clothes. No time for any crap. Let's go."

I felt Ivan touch my shoulder. He leaned in close and spoke to me. "Don't worry, Niklaus. I'll see you soon."

My stomach was starting to knot. "Promise you'll see me soon. Promise everything."

"Of course I do."

"Say it."

"I promise everything."

I felt his hand lift from my shoulder. "Niklaus. Niklaus, don't worry. I'll be with you soon." And that was that. Those were the last words I heard from Ivan. I was guided quickly to the door.

The clinic smelt like Gerard Simon. Clean paper and wine. His touch was everywhere, quietly nasty. Deceptive and angry.

They said they were going to exchange my eyes. That I was donating them and in turn helping myself return to normality. But I was not a donor and they weren't here to make things better. They were here to harvest.

"We'll take you into prolonged sleep," said Gerard Simon. "In a couple of days you'll wake up. New eyes. No pain."

"But what if – "

"What if, what if. It's not a multiple choice. It's what we're going to do. Finish."

"I just thought that – "

"Yeah, whatever." His voice was quieter, he was already walking away. There was no time for any more questions. The team promptly went to work on my no-pain solution.

"Prolonged sleep" meant forty-eight hours of semi-consciousness. It was like a sticky, wet blanket had been thrown over my eyes and mind.

For hours at a time I felt I was on the brink of coming back to consciousness. And then I'd hear the sounds of my intravenous pump as it stirred into life. *Clickclickclickclick – mmmmmmmmm.* Periodic doses of sedation.

It came to be one of the most horrifying sounds I had ever heard. It meant that in a few minutes I would slip back into the pit. And no amount of mute screaming would help.

Often I could feel my muscles straining. But I knew I wasn't moving. All my joints ached and my throat was constantly heavy with spit.

And Gerard Simon was there. Sweeping in and out of my room. I imagined him standing over me, rubbing his hands together. Oily blood seeped from under his fingernails. When he smiled, it was Yosman's smile. Small and mean. Then he would have one hand on a bottle of cheap tequila, the other clenched in a white-knuckled fist.

I was deep in the nightmare. Their sedation and my imagination were plotting against me. Only the whispers held me up, stopped me from sinking deeper into the pit. The whispers were everywhere. Crawling under my wet and sticky blanket. "Specific mutation sequencing ... ocular reflex circuitry ... cross-match protocols ... retinal protein cloning ..."

From that time onwards I noticed very distinctly that everything took the form of words. There were no more colours, no ideas. Only words. They came to me as whispers, spoken directly above my head.

The whispers were like lifelines pulling me back to reality. After the clinic, they became a tightrope on which I balanced my life.

I was dumped on a mid-city street, quite literally, after they had finished with me. They had my eyes, I had theirs. It was all very unceremonious, I guess the heavy rain was making them rush. Quickly they took me out of the van and then drove away. That was the end of it.

I looked carefully around me. No matter how hard I concentrated, the effects of the change weren't there. It was an effort for me to feel any relief. Two days without real sleep had exhausted me. With all the resolve I had left, I started a slow trek to Ivan's studio.

"Old endings, new beginnings," as Ivan would say. Despite my fatigue I managed a smile. I wondered if there was a situation to which a Polish saying couldn't be applied.

The studio was full of whispers, but Ivan was not there. And had not been there for some time. For an instant I was afraid. Scared that my choice to go to the clinic had changed the way Ivan felt about me. The way *he* saw *me*. Then the scattered brushes, burnt paintings and broken equipment told me I was afraid for the wrong reasons.

I walked around his studio, listening to the rain. Listening to my footsteps. I remembered how Yosman had circled me as I sat on Ivan's couch. But the couch had been moved. It was up against the door like a barricade. A barricade that hadn't worked.

And there was a single whisper over and over again in the studio. It was the smell of exertion and sweat. And of pain and fear. The smell of begging for an end to the madness lingered on my tongue, so I could taste nothing else.

I crashed to the floor. I didn't understand, and I didn't want to try. I just wanted to lie on Ivan's couch. I wanted to pretend he was standing behind me and I could turn around and see him working at another painting.

I wanted to be weak so the guilt couldn't find me. So the horror of being alone would pass by. I wanted to be weak. I wanted to sleep. But I wasn't allowed to.

Rest was for the innocent, and I was guilty of something I didn't fully understand. I desperately wanted to find out what I had done. Why Ivan was gone.

I searched for every sound. And like strange trails of blood there were other whispers around the studio. I followed them in all directions.

Among the painters and artists there wasn't the slightest noise. Nor among the members of the Polish community. Only the newspapers made the vaguest sounds, and these sounds came to be the most fantastic knot of ignorance and irony. Ivan didn't even get a mention in an obituary, while Yosman got the headlines daily. And quite a bit more coverage after he started telling all the names he knew.

The newspapers didn't want to report what happened to people like Ivan or me. They wanted to generate interesting headlines. "Subterranean Military Outrage". "Underworld Bio-Harvest Clinic". They quoted Biocircuit Production Laws like it was a good substitute for real reporting. Gerard Simon's name never came up. Yosman wasn't that stupid.

Somewhere in an obscure business journal an editorial was printed. It looked to be a standard piece on an apparently unrelated issue. A small European firm was set to storm the arms market with the sale of its latest fighter prototype to the North Korean Airforce, "the most refined heat-sensitive assault plane ever". Perhaps I was the only one to see the link, or feel it.

I'd had enough. *I am no more for listening to this.* Ivan's simple words spoke perfectly of my frustration and resignation. There was truth to be found. Somewhere. Like drops of blood in the sea.

I was glad Ivan was not mentioned. I didn't want to remember him that way, his name smudged over cheap paper.

I wanted to remember him painting in flickering lamplight. I wanted to remember him spreading the colours with his fingers. Stretching out like a cat after every painting session. Skipping rope before going to bed.

Ivan, the steelworks and the rain. My broken triad. Now there's only the rain. Only and always.

I still like to listen. I feel less cheated when I don't have to look.

My future is one word after another. A string of whispers, black over white. There will be no paintbrushes or canvases. Through my new eyes the world is flatter and older, less vivid. The only true colours remain in my memory.

All I have left are the words.

You could sleep even on the rocks. What is the feeling with you this morning? Pah, everything! You choose, chicken soup or chicken soup? Niklaus. Niklaus, don't worry. I'll be with you soon.

Afterword

I love writing. I enjoy doing it in a number of styles and genres. Science fiction is one of those genres. Unfortunately I'm not at liberty to predict what I'll write next, SF or non-SF, because the ideas just come into my head. Mainly I just write down whatever's there.

In many ways, writing SF releases me from the "real-life" constrictions inherent in other genres, be they history, geography, logic or even gravity. But at the same time it requires of me a believable fiction – a realism I can't get from just looking out the window. That's the challenge of writing SF.

When I was younger I spent a fair amount of time writing stories. The protagonist in "Everything" seems to be an amalgam of the young heroes that used to feature prominently in those stories. Perhaps a stronger sense of reality has caught up with me in that I have made Niklaus more the victim and less the hero. Then again, it might just be a pessimistic phase I'm going through.

White Christmas

Sean Williams

Sean Williams *started writing science fiction and horror four years ago and has since had over three dozen short stories published in various anthologies (including* Writers of the Future Volume IX, Terror Australis, *and* Intimate Armageddons) *and magazines* (Aboriginal SF, Bloodsongs, Aurealis, Eidolon, EOD *and others). He is coauthor, with Shane Dix, of the first three novels of the* Cogal *series.*

When not writing, he pursues his other major hobby (music) by working in a compact disc shop, studying part-time, and collecting the works of the late Frank Zappa. He was born in Whyalla and currently lives in Adelaide (which he destroys every now and again, just to relieve tension).

It was as he remembered it, except for the snow. Coming around the final bend in the winding road, with the bare shoulder of the mountain on his right and a yawning gulf on his left, Stewart slowed as the shack finally came into view. The tiny building was crowded by half-hearted scrub, through which a narrow driveway led to a dark veranda. He swung the Toyota as close to the front door as he could, and killed the engine.

The shack was uninhabited; that was obvious even from the outside, and expected. Owned by Jack and Debbie Barnard, property developers from Sydney, it stood empty for all but six weeks of every year, when it served as a private retreat. With no phone, fax or modem, television, radio or satellite dish, its isolation was complete. The nearest town, Blinman, was a half-hour drive back down the hill – too far to be a temptation, but near enough for emergencies. The shack was, as the owners liked to say, perfect for philosophers, writers, and honeymooners.

Stewart Danby didn't smile at the last. He had come alone, this time. Jacqui was back in Adelaide ... in what was *left* of Adelaide, rather ... and he was trying not to think about that.

Leaning forward over the steering-wheel, fatigue making his hands shake, he studied the ground around the Toyota. The sun was setting, filling the Flinders Ranges with gold and blood, deepening slowly to royal purple. Drifts of snow lay like scraps of cloth in the lee of the building and in the shallow troughs of the rising hillside, but otherwise the area seemed clear. He took a deep breath and opened the car door, leaving the keys in the ignition.

The shack's single door was locked, but he managed to prise open a loose rear window. The air inside was stuffy and hot; the coolness of the mid-summer twilight had yet to penetrate the thick stone walls. Opening the front door from within, he went back outside to unload the car.

Three boxes of canned food he had stolen from a supermarket were followed by a sleeping-bag; a jerry-can of kerosene and two bottles of butane gas; a set of scuba gear with half-a-dozen extra bottles, also stolen; a box of gaffer tape; half a carton of cigarettes; coffee, sugar and powdered milk; and five bottles of scotch, one of which was already open.

By the time the Toyota was empty, the sun had set. The air of the hills stank of rotten eggs, an odour he had gradually become used to during the drive. After his exposure to the relatively untainted air inside the shack, however, it caught anew in the back of his throat. He drank from the open bottle of scotch, wincing; the fire of the spirit wasn't sufficient to overpower the stench, but it helped.

He stood for a moment under the pale, starry bowl, head tipped back, the scotch in one hand, a cigarette in the other. The deep valley below was in darkness. Above the opposite hills, the comet was rising. The feather of glowing smoke smudged the south-western sky like a fingerprint on a masterpiece.

He shivered, although it wasn't cold, and lowered his eyes.

Snow, sparkling faintly in the comet-light, had already settled on the pitted roof and bonnet of the car. Dropping the gearstick into neutral and disengaging the handbrake, he gave the bumper-bar a push with his foot and stepped clear. The car rolled backwards down the drive, across the winding road that had brought him to the shack, then disappeared suddenly over the lip of the chasm. A series of tinkling smashes accompanied its descent into darkness, followed by silence as thick as bedrock. There was no explosion.

He swigged from the bottle again and went inside.

The shack was furnished in old seventies pine, stained yellow by age and nicotine: two chairs, a sofa and a rickety table. Amateurish paintings in cheap frames cluttered the walls. The carpet was a mottled burgundy, frayed at the edges and sorely in need of replacement. Sagging bookcases full of cheap paperbacks, mostly science fiction, lined one wall. The opposite wall was one long window, hidden behind curtains. He tugged them open. The view was black, but he knew that it would be spectacular by daylight. The comet winked balefully at him, and he shut the curtains again.

Lighting the stove, he filled the kettle with rainwater and set it to boil. While he waited, he unpacked the tins of food. Apart from some chipped, mismatched crockery, the cupboards contained nothing but dust and fluff. The bench-tops were spotted with dead flies. He made a half-hearted attempt to clean away the evidence of emptiness, but gave up before he had finished. There was no point.

The kettle screeched plaintively, like a baby, and he made the coffee. Stirring the various powders into a muddy solution, he breathed the cleansing steam into his nostrils. The combination of dust and hydrogen sulphide was giving his sinuses hell, but there wasn't much he could do about it. With the coffee mug in one hand, he explored the rest of the shack.

The bathroom was a small cubicle next to the kitchen. It contained a primitive shower, with an instant gas heater powered by roof-mounted solar panels, and a tiny handbasin. The chemical toilet was a small plastic box in one corner, lid shut. Mould seeped down the walls like the shadows of stalactites. A tiny mirror hung on one wall, blotched white with soap. Exactly as he remembered it.

The single bedroom was bare apart from a coffin-like cupboard containing nothing but coathangers, and a stripped double bed. The mattress was stained brown and in the final stages of internal collapse. Again, the same as it had been. He recalled the time, five years earlier, when he and Jacqui had ...

No. He went back into the main room and found the half-empty bottle of scotch. He preferred cold blankness to the grief and pain that waited to claim him. He could feel it building, growing like a bubble deep in his throat. When it burst, as it surely would, he didn't think he would be able to survive. The shock was fading, so he had to feed the anaesthesia some other way. It was either that, or leave.

And he couldn't leave. No matter what perverse internal logic had led him here, he had to go with it. With nowhere else to go, and no way to get there, only the shack and the past were left to keep him company.

In activity there was relief. He opened two tins and cooked himself a simple casserole of meat and vegetables. He fussed with the burner, with the plates, took his time eating and washing the few dishes. The bottle emptied fast, and he opened another. The night deepened. He could feel the comet crossing the heavens above him; invisible through the ceiling, but still there. A primitive clock to measure the thickening of the night.

It became cold at last – a deep, desert cold. A pot-bellied

stove crouched in one corner of the main room, but he hadn't thought to bring wood. Lighting the kerosene heater, he chain-smoked, watched the purple flame flickering, and finished the second bottle.

When the sun eventually rose, it was pallid and less intense that it had been the previous day. The snow had tightened its grip on the valley overnight and reflected the myriad shades of dawn back at the cloudless sky.

Inside his mind, more memory than dream, another sun rose.

He was driving the Toyota back from Port Germein, where he had stayed the weekend with a cousin. He almost hadn't gone at all, but Jacqui had talked him into it.

"Just go, dammit. You need the break."

"But I've got work to do."

"Work? It's *Christmas*, Stew." She put her hands on her hips, resembling more than ever a cross brown bear. "No buts. You missed it last time and complained for a month. I don't want to listen to your whining again."

"I don't remember any whining."

"It was pathetic." A grin surfaced through the mock anger. "God knows I can't see the attraction in some cosmic ball of fluff, but I understand what it means to you. You've been up in the clouds for days now, thinking about it, so just get the hell out of here and take a look, okay?" She took his chin in one hand and kissed him on the lips: the quick peck that said she meant business. "Okay?"

She had been talking about the comet, of course – Ronson's Comet, which had reached perigee the previous autumn. In the city, the spectral visitor had been pale and foreshortened, a dusty smudge almost invisible through the wash of street-lights. Hamish, his cousin, had waxed lyrical about its beauty from the country, but Stewart had been too busy tying up a publishing deal to spare the time to travel to Port Germein, where Hamish lived.

And Jacqui had been right: he had regretted missing it. If perigee had come a single week later, he might have been able to arrange something, but it hadn't. When the comet had vanished behind the sun, he had cursed himself anyway for not taking the opportunity that Hamish had presented. He tried to resign himself to the fact that he had missed it, but with only partial success.

Then, after perihelion, the comet's orbit shifted – as a result of violent gas discharges from its unimaginable surface. The second perigee, scheduled for the middle of December, was even closer than the first. Earth, and Stewart Danby, had been given a second chance.

"Okay, okay." He capitulated gracelessly, feigning reluctance. Jacqui didn't want to come, he knew that, but he didn't want to seem too eager to go without her, either. Although he would miss her, her lack of enthusiasm would only dampen the experience.

He left the following Friday afternoon and arrived at Port Germein in time for a spectacular sunset. The small fishing town was lively with weekend tourists, who, like him, had fled the perpetual blindness of the city's light for the transparent skies of the country. The night was hot and clear, perfect for idle star-gazing. The local council had arranged a blackout, to aid the amateur observers.

Sharing a six-pack on Hamish's back veranda, Stewart watched the comet rise, knowing it would be a sight he would never forget.

Away from the city, its tail stretched across half the sky, nebulous but clear. Through binoculars, it looked like faintly glowing smoke, backlit by stars. He thought he detected colours in its feathery wake, but couldn't be certain.

"I doubt it," said Hamish, who had read a lot in the last few weeks and become assertively confident with his new knowledge. "Takes a spectrometer to pick out the elements. The naked eye just sees white."

There followed a discussion of the comet's origins, little of which was new to Stewart. It had drifted into the solar system from deep space, not from the Oört cloud. Unlike Halley's Comet, it was a new addition to the family of planets and only a temporary one. After perigee, it would swing out of the system, never to return.

"Show you something interesting," said Hamish, producing a magazine. Holding a lit cigarette lighter, he illuminated one glossy page. On it was printed a simple picture of the comet's altered orbit. "What does this look like?"

"A fish," said Stewart, and Hamish nodded. The sun was the fish's eye, the Earth a tiny dot in its tail.

"An *Ichthys*, more to the point." Hamish grinned wryly and extinguished the lighter. "Glad I'm not a Christian."

It took Stewart a moment to remember the word, and to realise what his cousin was suggesting. Comets were traditionally signs of doom and destruction; coming so close to the end of the millennium, their prophetic powers were augmented. That Ronson's Comet was further coupled with a common symbol of the Christian saviour augured the Apocalypse, Judgement Day.

"Maybe you should become one," he joked. "A Christian, I mean. Before it's too late."

Hamish snorted in the darkness. "Crap."

"No, really, doesn't it seem a little strange? It did change course, after all." The question begged to be asked. "Maybe we didn't get the message first time around."

"Coincidence, Stew. That's all."

Stewart smiled in the star-spattered darkness. Hamish was right, of course, but he wondered how many New Age evangelists would profit from the comet's timely appearance. "Five to one says you're wrong."

"You're on, sucker."

The weekend passed quickly. Perigee had been the previous Wednesday, but the comet showed no immediate signs of decreasing in magnitude. Tiny sparks seemed to twinkle in its tail, glinting, insubstantial and short-lived. Boulders of dislodged ice, suggested Hamish, although he admitted that he had neither seen the phenomenon before nor read of it. Stewart wasn't convinced, but kept his opinion to himself; to have witnessed the phenomenon alone was enough. He didn't need a knowledge of pyrotechnics to enjoy fireworks.

Reluctant to leave, he delayed his departure as long as possible. The comet was hypnotic, beguiling, a drop of dye in the clear water of mundane, modern life. Eventually he drove out of Port Germein at four o'clock on the Monday morning, knowing he would later regret the lack of sleep, but glad that he had made the effort to be there, to stay those extra few hours.

It was at this point that the dream began.

Half way to Adelaide, with the comet low ahead of him and the sun rising on his left, he stopped to rest by the side of the highway. A fatigue hangover had begun somewhere behind his eyeballs, and he relished the chance to close his eyes.

A sudden strong gust of wind made him squint at the lightening sky. Clouds were rolling in from the south-west with astonishing speed. Pure white, but as large as thunderheads, they bulked over the horizon, growing larger as he watched. The wind picked up sharply, and he headed back to the

Toyota for shelter. There was electricity in the air, a powerful aura of impending disaster.

He started the car and pulled back onto the highway, leaving the lights on. The shadow of the clouds covered him, bringing a semblance of night back with it. The wind became more insistent, tugging the Toyota to one side.

His radio, tuned to a country station, crackled in mid-chorus and died. The shadow deepened; behind him, the last segment of pale blue sky vanished.

He stared in absolute astonishment as, maybe for the first time ever in that part of Australia, it began to snow.

He awoke gasping for breath, momentarily disoriented. Then he remembered where he was, and what he was doing there. He was at the Barnards' shack in the Flinders Ranges, and he had come there to … what? Forget? Hide?

Die?

Staggering out of the chair, wincing at the light that stabbed through the gaps between the curtains, he found the scuba gear, put on the rubber facemask and twisted a knob. High-pressure air hissed into his open mouth. He lay back on the floor of the shack and sucked in the sweet coolness.

The muzziness in his head gradually faded. He switched off the valve and removed the mask. The air in the shack was thick and pungent; more than ever the stench of rotten eggs filled his nostrils. Breathing heavily through his open mouth, he rummaged in a box for the gaffer tape.

Then, slowly and carefully, he sealed every gap in the shack's stone walls: window-frames, air-vents, cracks under doors. Everything.

When he had finished, he collapsed with his face pressed against a dirty windowpane, his chest rising and falling in spasms. Outside, the atmosphere seemed unnaturally dense and yellowish. Although the sky was still cloudless, the snow-cover was thicker than it had been the night before. It now piled in drifts against the walls of the shack, and he was reminded of the red weed in H. G. Wells' *The War of the Worlds*. The snow had turned the valley into an alien landscape: moon-like, with gentle curves and featureless bulges in places of more earthly scenery.

The bubble in his throat was growing, making it even more difficult to breathe. With clumsy fingers he turned on the scuba gear again and flooded the room with fresh air.

Three days had passed since that early morning when he had first gaped incredulously at the white powder batting in flurries at the Toyota. The forecast the previous night had said nothing about storms, let alone snow. It was a warm summer night; he couldn't imagine where such a mass of super-cold air had come from, or how the snow survived the fall to the ground without melting into rain. The only places in Australia where conditions allowed the freezing of water in any form, as far as he knew, were the Snowy Mountains and the south of Tasmania, both during winter. Not South Australia, the driest state, in the middle of summer ...

Ahead, the road had vanished under a thin carpet of white, and he slowed the car automatically. There seemed to be no slippage, however; his wheels gripped the road surface as well as ever, which seemed strange. Surely melting snow was more treacherous than water? And the stuff wasn't even sticking to the windscreen, as he'd assumed it would.

The last stop before entering the northern edge of the city was Port Wakefield. He pulled into a service station, partly to refuel, mostly to assess the situation, but the attendant knew as little as he did. Snow was falling, impossible snow, and the radio frequencies were still swamped by interference. There was no chance of an updated weather report until the storm cleared.

It seemed safe to assume that the freak weather had hit the city, and he wondered whether Jacqui could shed some light on it. She had spent some years in Europe before moving to Australia, so her knowledge of snowstorms was bound to be greater than his. He didn't even know if it was safe to drive, or whether tyre chains were required. Traffic around Christmas was heavy, and he didn't want to be caught in a pile-up.

But when he tried to ring Jacqui from a public phone, the line was dead. The last time he had spoken to her had been from Hamish's home the previous night, and nothing had been amiss. A line must have come down since then, probably as a result of the storm.

He got back into the car and continued on his way. Not long afterwards the snow stopped falling, but the thick, fairy-floss clouds remained and the radio stayed dead. The closer he came to the city, the thicker the ground-cover became; even the tyre-tracks of the cars preceding his seemed faint. Slowly he decreased his speed until he was travelling at barely above sixty kilometres per hour.

Just outside the first main intersection, the snow became too thick to pass. A number of cars blocked the highway, making further progress impossible. Pulling to a halt, he walked to join the others who had gathered on the roadside, scuffing incredulously at the snow. It crunched faintly beneath his feet, like sand.

"This is just great," said one woman, a bedraggled mother of four children who squealed and squawked from a nearby station-wagon. "My mother's expecting us this morning, and we're already an hour late."

"Can't get past it," said a middle-aged man with a biker's

beard and dirty leathers. He radiated an aura of patient, if faintly puzzled, pragmatism, and Stewart found his attitude calming. The biker gestured at the bank of snow in their path. "I've just come from further on. The traffic's bogged in solid. Take a tractor to shift it."

"Maybe it levels out. We might be able to force our way – "

"Lady, it was up to my waist when I turned back, and getting deeper. Unless you've got a bulldozer handy, I can't see how you're gonna get through it."

"What the hell are we supposed to do, then?"

"Try another way in, I guess." The biker scratched at his beard. "Come down via the hills maybe."

The woman was not happy. "Forget it. I'm going to wait. The council can get their act together."

The biker smiled. "Maybe, but I don't think snowploughs are all that common round here."

"Any idea where it came from?" Stewart asked.

"The greenhouse effect," said the woman. "It fell through a hole in the ozone layer."

The biker looked unconvinced. "Beats me, to be honest. It hit right out of the blue. No warning, no nothing." He lashed out with a leather riding-boot, sending a snowdrift scattering. "But that's not what really worries me."

"What, then?"

"Touch it, and you'll see what I mean."

Stewart hesitated, then stooped and plunged his hand into the drift at his feet. To his surprise, the snow wasn't cold; not even cool. It was as warm as the earth it covered, and felt gritty on his palm and fingertips.

"It's not cold," said the biker, "it's not melting, and I doubt you could build a snowman out of it. If it's *really* snow, I'll eat my leathers."

Standing up and glancing around, Stewart tried to make sense of the phenomenon. Snow lay everywhere: a thick blanket of white, definitely becoming deeper in the direction of Adelaide. It hung from trees like scraps of torn sheets, too unusual to be truly beautiful. If it wasn't snow, he thought, then perhaps it was ash. Had there been some sort of volcanic explosion in Adelaide's vicinity? As far as he knew there were no volcanoes, active or dead, for many hundreds of kilometres, although the city did lie on top of a fault line ...

"I'm heading for the hills," said the biker, stamping off to his bike. "No point standing around here all day."

Stewart agreed and went back to the Toyota, leaving the mother alone to deal with her kids.

Two hours later, coming down the last leg of the Great Eastern Freeway, he passed the biker going back up. Recognising the car, the biker flagged him down.

"Don't bother. Blocked that way too. Worse, if anything."

"Shit." That explained why he had seen few cars coming either way, even though it was close to peak-hour. "Where now?"

"Me, I'm going back to the lookout. Might be able to see something from there."

Stewart followed the motorbike back up the freeway to a concrete car park hollowed out of the chest of the foothills. There, he produced the binoculars he had taken with him to study the comet and turned them on the landscape below.

Through the clouds, which hung low and heavy over the hills, he could see little. Handing the binoculars to the biker, he leaned forward over the concrete barrier, trying to pierce the cloud-cover by sheer force of will.

The clouds parted for an instant, allowing them an unobstructed view.

"Jesus *Christ*," whispered the biker.

"What? What can you see?"

Wordlessly, the biker shook his head and handed the binoculars back to him.

Stewart focused the lenses, swept his amplified stare across the suburbs and streets of the city. White, everywhere, just white. No details. It looked as though fog or heavy mist had covered the city, obscuring it from sight. But it wasn't mist.

"Look at the city centre," suggested the biker.

Landmarks lay buried beneath the white pancake. He didn't realise he had found the city centre until he recognised the silhouette of the State Bank building, the tallest in Adelaide. It too was shrouded in white, as though a cloth had been draped over it, but it didn't look as tall as it should have been. The buildings around it were similarly foreshortened, and some appeared to be missing altogether. He frowned: the snow couldn't be that thick, could it?

As he watched, puzzled, the State Bank building slumped and fell over, melting into the snow like a spear of ice-cream under the hot sun.

"Oh my god," he breathed.

"The city's going under," said the biker. "It's burying it."

"But ..." Stewart lowered the binoculars. "That's ..."

"I'm getting out of here. Something weird's going on, and I don't like it."

"The snow ...?"

"It's *not* snow, I know that much." The biker raised his nose to sniff the wind. "Can you smell it? The air is turning."

Stewart found an edge to the air, like rotten eggs, blowing up from the foothills.

"My wife works in the city," he said, a cold weight beginning to settle in his stomach.

"You got any kids?" asked the biker.

He shook his head.

"I've got three." A dirty hand flapped at the terrible whiteness. "Somewhere under *that*."

"You're not going to leave them?"

The biker worried his beard with one hand. "If they're okay, then they can look after themselves. If they're not, there's nothing I can do."

"We have to *try*, don't we?"

The biker looked uncomfortable for a moment. Then, without replying, he strode back to the bike and kicked it into life. The roar of the engine leaped from the hills as he sped back to the highway.

Stewart stayed until the cloud-cover closed again, cutting off the view of the city. There was nothing new to be seen, apart from the gentle, silent collapse of the city centre; just an endless snowfield that stretched as far as the sea. No details, no signs of life.

His stomach gnawed at itself as he drove on down the freeway. The snow piled higher and higher, until he rounded a corner and reached a solid wall of the stuff with a handful of cars parked in front of it. The bike leaned on its stand among them, and Stewart was gratified to see it, although the biker himself was nowhere to be seen.

A clot of people had gathered near the blockage. Walking up to them, Stewart addressed a short, balding man who seemed to have elected himself leader.

"The biker. Where did he go?"

The man pointed over the snow-dune. "In there. With Gary."

Footprints led over the dune. Thanking the bald man, he followed the double tracks. The snow was at least three metres deep in places and as hard to walk through as soft sand. As the tracks wandered on, the dunes piled higher, licking at the rock walls where the freeway had been cut out of the hills. An icing-sugar canyon. He shivered, although it still wasn't cold; it was, in fact, oppressively hot. The smell of rotten eggs was strong in the still, stifled air.

He turned a bend and caught sight of the biker and the man called Gary. They were standing not much further on, looking at something on the ground between them. He called to them, and both glanced at him in surprise.

Gary was tall, with a pot-gut and thinning black hair. As Stewart approached, he realised that the man's face was as white as the snow around them.

"You don't want to see this," said the biker.

Stewart forced his way between them and stared at what lay at their feet. At first, all he saw was a dash of red in the ubiquitous white, until the details fell into place.

It was the body of a woman, partly buried. Her clothes were gone, and her staring eyes were full of empty accusation. The condition of her body suggested a violent, hideous passing – or subsequent mutilation.

"There's a car up ahead," said Gary. "Abandoned."

"Someone dumped her here?" asked Stewart, forcing the words through the gorge rising in his throat.

"We don't think so. She must have crawled from it, got buried, and suffocated. If I hadn't tripped over her, we never would've found her."

"But who ...?" He gestured at the corpse, lost for words.

"Skinned her? Look closely."

Reluctantly, Stewart did so. The snow lay across her vivid flesh like ribbons, or ropes. More: it seemed to be digging in, somehow, as though she might yet struggle free. This impression alone was enough to disturb him, until he noticed something else.

"It … it's moving!"

The biker nodded. "It's *eating* her."

Stewart's stomach spasmed. Staggering backwards, he clutched his mouth and simultaneously wiped at the snow that had settled on his skin. "Oh, Jesus …"

The biker put a steadying hand on his shoulder and smiled without humour.

"It probably won't hurt you," he said. "Or us. We're still alive, you see."

Stewart swallowed his nausea and forced his hands to be still, cursing his foolishness. He had been exposed to the snow on several occasions and it hadn't harmed him. "But … I don't understand."

"The car," said Gary, "was almost gone. It looked … dissolved. The snow was stripping it back to nothing."

The biker nodded, and gestured at the body. "Same with her. She's just raw material."

"For what?"

The biker waved a hand at the canyon of snow. "For whatever this stuff really is."

"Machines," said Gary. "Nano-machines, or something. Designed to dig in and separate the useful stuff from the rest. Like ants, but smaller."

"Is that possible?" asked the biker.

"I can't see why not."

Stewart could feel panic rising through his confusion. He allowed himself to be led away from the body, back up the freeway.

"The comet," he whispered, half to himself.

Gary nodded, as though he had already considered the idea. "It's possible."

"Aliens?" The biker raised his eyebrows.

"Or something non-intelligent. This stuff could be a life-form, some sort of mindless bug."

"Do you think so?"

"No. It hit the city dead on. That suggests a purposeful intent."

"Maybe they home in on metal?"

"Or high-density electric fields." Gary shrugged at the biker's question. "I don't know. But if it *is* aliens, then this could be just the beginning – phase one, if you like. Maybe they're going to build something next. Or take over."

The biker nodded slowly. "The air's starting to smell bad."

"Exactly. Depending on how much of this stuff there is, world-wide, it would be fairly easy to change the environment. And if the snow's self-replicating, then it'd be even easier. Once the bugs are loose, there'd be no stopping them."

"How long?" Stewart heard the question before realising that he had asked it. A scream was building at the back of his throat, and he swallowed to force it down.

Gary shrugged. "I don't know. I'm not a scientist."

"You'll have to ask the aliens," suggested the biker. "If they exist."

They walked back to the cars in solemn silence. The walls of the canyon loomed over them, higher than before. In the short time they had been studying the woman's gory corpse, the snow had thickened.

When they reached the last snow-dune, Gary turned to them and, as though he regretted his earlier words, said:

"Remember, it's only a theory. I could be wrong."

"Then why haven't we seen any planes?" asked the biker. "And why aren't the radios working?"

"I don't know. But I don't think we should start a panic over what might turn out to be nothing."

"Nothing?" The biker shook his head. "We've been invaded by *something*, haven't we? Surely we should try to fight back?"

"How? How do you fight *snow*?"

Stewart collapsed into the seat of the Toyota, his mind whirling. The idea of aliens invading the planet was too crazy to be true, and yet it made a horrible kind of sense: to hit the cities first, to use a widespread plague of machines to contaminate the environment, to hide in a comet, where no one would ever think to look ...

The comet had swung past the Earth once, perhaps to survey the territory, then had changed course during perihelion. The whip of the sun's gravity had dragged it back for one more visit, to drop its deadly cargo into the atmosphere. Maybe just a handful of snow-particles at first, breeding, self-replicating in the upper altitudes, until enough existed to cover the major cities of the Earth. And then it had started falling: snowflakes, innocent and unexpected, *everywhere*, unstoppable.

It did make sense. And, even if the theory was wrong, the facts remained, indisputable. Adelaide was buried and crumbling beneath the snow. Judging by the rate the woman's body had dissolved, the city wouldn't last long.

He glanced at his watch; the storm had ended just four hours earlier. It seemed like a lifetime. His hands shook with delayed shock; a coldness spread through his mind, numbing the part of him that wanted to scream. Through the growing fog, it became, strangely, easier to think. Although the terrible coldness appalled him, he knew that it was a defence mechanism: he needed to think rationally if he was going to survive.

If Jacqui was still alive, then there was nothing he could do to reach her. Better to assume that she was dead, that everyone in the city was dead. And, as the snow of the initial fall spread and grew, the area around the city wouldn't be safe for long. His weekend of comet-spotting might have saved his life in the short term, but how long would it be before the snow spread to encompass neighbouring towns?

And how long before the entire world succumbed?

With no clear destination in mind, certain only that he had to move somewhere, he started the car and headed back up the freeway.

The last bottle of compressed air emptied with the fifth bottle of scotch, and he was down to his last cigarette. It was four days since the snow had started to fall. The roof was sagging under the weight of the stuff that had settled upon it; white tendrils crept through the gaffer tape, wormed across the worn carpet.

It was Christmas Day, and he had run out of anaesthetic.

As the bubble burst and grief poured in to fill the empty space in his chest, he realised that this was what he had been waiting for all along. This was why he had come back to the Barnards' shack, where he and Jacqui had spent their first week of marriage together. Not to forget or to hide, but to grieve. To say goodbye.

The last time he had spoken to Jacqui, the telephone line from Port Germein had been faint but clear. He had been amazed at how much he had missed her, even though he'd only been away two nights. Now all he had was a memory of her voice. The woman he loved was gone. The assumption had been easy to make, but the realisation of the fact had taken time.

Tears burned his eyes. He didn't try to fight them any more. Maybe he had been waiting for them to come. The pain made it easier to cut free from the world that had ended and to which he could never return.

By the time his spasm of grief ebbed, half an hour had passed. The air was thickening again, curdling before his very eyes.

Rising from the chair, he drew back the curtains. The valley and its native scrub had disappeared. In its place was a world drained of colour. The snow had formed delicate spires and towers, upraised to greet the sun. The alien forest was still and silent, but he could sense a vitality stirring through it, as though the snow itself was alive.

The Earth wasn't dead, but *changed*. It no longer belonged to its previous owners. Already, he felt like a trespasser. An unwanted intruder, witnessing the birth of a new world. He wondered if he was the only one.

On the heels of this thought, there came a noise from the rear of the shack: a rattle of rocks, loud in the stillness of the valley. Turning his back to the view, he went to the kitchen window and peered out.

Something was moving down the hill. The creature looked at first like a giant spider, with legs over five metres long, crawling ponderously towards the cabin. As white as the snow it traversed, it moved with all the precision of a surgical instrument. Limbs swivelled and folded neatly to match niches and holds buried beneath the snow. There was no wastage of movement, not the slightest hesitation or inefficiency. He was unable to decide whether it was a machine or a living creature.

When it came to a halt not five metres away, the legs collapsed along its sides and it became a giant flea, two metres high. Stewart could see no eyes in the knobbled, ugly "face", but sensed that it was watching the shack intently, as though waiting for him to make a move.

"How long?" he had asked Gary, just days earlier. He remembered the biker's reply:

"You'll have to ask the aliens."

If phase one – the snow – had already ended, then the creature in front of him was part of phase two. Probably the creatures were not aliens themselves, but motile drones programmed to scour the surface of the planet. Robots. The colonists themselves would come later, perhaps resurrected from frozen genetic material, to assume their roles as the new masters of the Earth. And then the invasion would be complete.

An invasion without war. Just the silent, peaceful fall of snowflakes.

The process might already have been repeated on a thousand worlds, and might be on a thousand yet to come. Wherever the comet passed, it would leave behind it the legacy of an unknown race, spreading like a cancer from star to star. How many other civilisations had died in order that this one might live? How long would it be before the comet encountered a race that was able to fight back?

The creature didn't move. It seemed puzzled, as though uncertain what to make of the shack and its occupant; as though its programmers had not told it how to deal with a belligerent native.

Maybe, thought Stewart, the conquering race had never encountered another civilisation anywhere in its travels. Maybe it had assumed that none such was to be found anywhere in the galaxy, and that all suitable planets were therefore fit for terraforming. Maybe the destruction of the human Earth had been a mistake. And maybe it wasn't too late, after all ...

He guessed he wouldn't have to wait long for phase three. For one wild moment, he imagined that he could survive to explain the mistake – if he rationed his food and breathed shallowly, if he could keep the snow from destroying the shack around him. There had to be others who had survived, like him, by holing up and doing nothing.

The creature unfolded its legs and moved towards him.

He backed away from the window, thinking of the last thing Gary had said:

"How do you fight *snow?*"

The answer, of course, was that you couldn't. It had taken him four days alone in the shack to come to terms with the fact.

He opened the cocks on the butane bottles and waited until the smell of hydrogen sulphide had vanished, swamped by another, more potent smell.

The sound of glass shattering came from the kitchen, followed by the breaking of solid stone.

He closed his eyes and lit the cigarette.

Afterword

Speculative fiction (which includes science fiction and horror) appeals to me because of its incredible diversity. No other genre has the freedom to explore such wildly varied scenarios and subjects: alien environments, or ones identical to ours; time-scales that encompass the ultimate destiny of the human race, or an afternoon in Melbourne; monsters too terrible to be imagined, or the small horrors that leak from the human psyche. Under the umbrella of SF, every possible universe is a stage, and literally anything can be an actor upon it.

The impact of the alien upon the normal is a core scenario in SF, but what may seem normal to one person may be quite alien to another. Having lived in Adelaide for most of my life, I have rarely seen snow and found the possibility of a White Christmas in Adelaide worth exploring. At the same time, recent developments in nano-technology and the possibility of using it for warfare demanded a story. It seemed logical to combine the two ideas. (The alternatives, nuclear winter and the return of the ice age, have been well-used already.) What resulted was an image quite different from the fairytale, white-blanketed Yule perpetuated by the media.

Malcolm and the Intergalactic Slug-suckers

Paul Voermans

Paul Voermans *is Dutch-Indonesian. He was born in Gippsland in 1960 and currently lives in Melbourne again after several years abroad. At sixteen he attended a science fiction writers' workshop during the school holidays; and his first science fiction story, written there, was published in* The View from the Edge, *edited by George Turner. Since then his stories have appeared in both Australian and English magazines. His two science fiction novels,* And Disregards the Rest *and* The Weird Colonial Boy, *are published by Victor Gollancz, London. He has ten years' experience as an actor, including a lead role in the ABC TV series* Trapp, Winkle and Box, *and has exhibited performance masks at the National Gallery of Victoria and taught mime at the Victorian College of the Arts. Fish fascinate him.*

INSTRUCTION MANUAL FOR HYPERCORIC ATTENUATOR ZX4900

INSERT IN DRIVE AND TOUCH ANY STYLEPAD KEY

INTRODUCTION:

Congratulations! You, like millions of others, have entered the wonderful HyperCoric *universe. Whatever environment you inhabit, however many other brands you have tried, no matter what organs you have adopted or borrowed or had genegrafted before birth, there is only one type of attenuware to suit all your needs –* HyperCoric.

IMPORTANT:

For users within 50 parsecs of the Hercules Cluster, please make sure the blue jeffness hatch is open and the invective disk (puce) is inserted before activation.

CAUTION:

- *Fill sarcasm points with lint only after greasing nipples.*
- *Do not pour water on treenun.*
- *Belt pre-attenuator firmly when in transit to prevent*

saddening tropic nodules. If any form of melancholia occurs, call your dealer immediately.

NOT INCLUDED WITH THIS PRODUCT:

Terrestrial footware, micropond, lithoprops, schizophrene or bottled knickers. Check with your HyperCoric *dealer for these accessories.*

GENERAL INSTRUCTIONS:

Meet Malcolm. He's your model HyperCoric *Attenuator* ZX4900 *user. Listen to Malcolm and get the most out of your* ZX4900. *Touch stylepad* DEPTH *key twice to get to know him.*

You know, my olds reckon I'm the biggest nong in the Claimed Universe. Freak of nature, born to bumble. Just yesterday Dad was ranting about the mess I'd made of the laundry stripping the dog down for a clean. "His tail's wagging all over my washing! How can the poor thing run around like that?"

When I turned to Mum she hardly looked up from her work-station. "Do what your father tells you," she said, and stuck her head back into the HomeOffice hologram. I only ever see the back of her these days.

Sometimes I just have to get away. And since my Hyper-Coric Attenuator ZX4900 was due, I climbed onto the roof to wait for it.

Now, the roof is my favourite spot. I'd grown the little platform from a bean a few years back. Up there I found one of those sunsets that almost proves fairies do exist: so delicate you'd swear some geek in chiffon with a wand could float down and grant you the usual backfiring wishes. I stared out across other roofs and pads, listening to the springtime burps of the wastelizards and sniffing the lovely evening pittosporum – but I felt tense. The delivery squatter might not excrete the box gently on the pad, I worried. It might not come at all! I kept asking my book the time. It kept making dumb jokes about Swedish parking inspectors. I was just about to toss it to the lizards when I noticed a spangly orange fog to my left.

I turned.

It turned with me.

I stopped turning (I was getting dizzy).

Out of the air a nose materialised.

A faceless schnozz, I thought. I'm going bananas.

"Gn nyu ee-aw bme?" said the nose.

I almost fell off the platform.

"Gn nyu *ee-aw* bme? Gn. Nyu *ee-aw* bme?"

Can you hear me? "Yes!" I said.

"Gwdf. Nnw kuw unn me nzzz."

I hesitated to do as it asked. For one thing the nzzz needed a blwww.

"NNnn!"

"Okay, okay! I'll do it now!" I reached for it and I missed, swiping it with my sleeve, accidental-like. Then, as you do with a nose, I grabbed it between index and forefinger and pulled.

I slipped. Practically off the roof.

The nose berated me. I sighed. There was nothing else for it. Gritting my teeth, I stuck my fingers up its nostrils and wrenched.

A cry of pain vibrated down my fingers, and through the spangly mist came the most degenerate character I have ever had the rotten luck to lay eyes upon. Not only was he preternaturally wasted but every normal bodily groove was bruise-coloured, as though he'd just escaped from a hospital or someplace worse. Each pore was a blackhead. He looked sad.

No wonder, I reckoned.

"You must not use your attenuator," he whispered hoarsely, spitting all over me in his desperation. "Don't even switch it on!"

With that he vanished. He left me with sputum on my face and bogans on my sleeve and fingers. He left me scared as anything. But not by his warning. I was worried that I was nuts.

VITAL NOTE:

If the seal on the instruction package is broken, DO NOT VIEW FURTHER. *Your disk could harbour viral agents. Please email the number on the outside of the box immediately. If Malcolm acts strangely or anything unlikely has occurred already,* DISREGARD COMPLETELY. *These are instructions from a viral disk which you cannot trust to describe the correct use of* HyperCoric *equipment.*

As it turned out, the company squatter did deliver the attenuator that day. But I didn't open it. Just in case I *wasn't* nuts.

When Malcolm opens the box the first thing he notices is the instruction disk you are now viewing. He pops it into the drive and views it all the way through *before attempting to assemble his* ZX4900 *attenuator.*

In the end I gave in. I had saved for nearly a year for this. I opened the box.

Now, Malcolm takes the pre-attenuator nodule, makes sure the solar line is made spunky, and performs all the tasks shown in Fig. 256 because he knows that instructions must be followed carefully at all times.

Naturally, I was so eager to get it going I skipped half the assembly stages, but everyone knows most of the SLUMFUNK.GRR files are only for the sort of person who needs reassurance on anything more complicated than a shoebox.

As I clicked the last mackerel ring into place and waited for the system to boot I felt a surge of somehow *right* anticipation, as though this was my destiny and some software was booting me, Malcolm Watkins, instead of just the attenuator. It was as uncanny as getting a gift you never knew you really wanted. Although we lived in a Naturals enclave and the biggest change my olds had given me was Koori gene enhancement (a bar mitzvah present), I felt like I was made for attenuation. Hardly likely unless they'd gone crazy and slipped GeneVector in my muesli. Well, I'd soon find out.

I gripped the attenuator grips. The sensors sensed me. I became thinner.

An orange mist filled my vision. Slowly I moved into it, and as my eyes passed the crucial point it gave way to a sky the colour of lime jelly.

I floated in it.

REMEMBER:

The HyperCoric ZX4900 *operates by thinning your space-time profile until probabilistic forces take over. That's why attenuatees are called "skinnies". You have "slipped between" the force-lines of space-time (please refer to the* HyperCoric *supplemental disk,* Space, Time and Your Big Feet, *for the physics involved) and into a reality where you are large and the stars are small. We all know the practical applications of this technology. Interstellar travel is the serious side to* HyperCoric. *This is the fun side. So relax. If you take a spill or feel like you're going too fast, just let go of the grips with both hands and the* ZX4900 *unit will send you straight back to your normal state. The fail-safe backups are too numerous to tell you about. Soon you'll be riding the stars with the best. Go for it!*

Fortunately it didn't feel like jelly. The wave-front slid beneath my board, a galaxy in the making, opalescent. Here I was huge, almost virtual, and the universe was just a series of mind-mushingly spectacular surf beaches. Stars for sand. Tides of gravity. I made a slight hop from one would-be spiral arm to another. It was so exciting that I couldn't help but speed up each time. I was headed for a dense cloud of stars, a difficult place to manoeuvre. If I could perform a half rotation before I arrived, the board's surface area would slow my descent into the cloud.

As they do in the movies, I pulled my knees up to my chest, then gave a small kick forward with both feet. Ah, what a champion: the board's momentum carried me too far and I performed a complete rotation – my head plunged into the nebula. Before the universe turned completely white with young stars I glimpsed a cluster of laughing faces on the cloud's edge. I felt their raucous noise flood into my arms through the attenuator's grips. Besides feeling hot with ridicule, it felt *weird* listening with my bones.

I paddled with a single hand back out of the cloud. The other skinnies were still laughing but I couldn't see them. Probably on the other side of the cloud, I thought. By sinking to my knees and paddling with alternate hands, making sure one hand always held a grip, I found I could get about with some control (if little dignity) on the cloud's outside.

I soon found the others.

They were the ugliest people I have ever met.

There were three of them. Stacker, Beluga, and The Walrus. This I could tell from the callsigns written across their foreheads. I could also see they wanted something, and it wasn't a game of bath quoits either.

Stacker was so fashion-engineered he was almost unrecognisable as human. It'd require expensive prostheses for him to get about in the normal universe. Apart from minor stuff like being orange and having drawers in his chest (guess what the handles were), Stacker was obviously named for the plug-in body units which he could rearrange himself. Or perhaps with trusted friends. So his head sported a foot instead of one ear, and he had arms instead of legs, and extra knees all over him. Organs were redistributed around his body seemingly at random and his buttocks sat on his shoulders like the pads people wore late last century. His head itself was placed where one hand ought to have been. Because of the extra cloned parts his gestures seemed faintly rude.

"What are you starin' at?" he said, through a flesh drawer instead of a mouth.

"Mmm," Beluga agreed, head rotating in disgust, then uncoiling with a snap. "He's rude on top of the ugly, eh boys?"

Beluga – I supposed – was a woman. Her skin was purple, the colour of fine ink, much darker than mine. Her pale yellow lips satirised fullness; like Stacker's they were replaceable. Her hair was short and pink and her lower face was webbed in silvery lines. She wore a frilly orange swimsuit harking back to the nineteen-fifties and over that a computer-generated holographic scribble, flicking and shimmering against the darkness of space like a neon sign advertising insanity by the bag. She was barefoot. Her eyes were dream-green. Beluga smiled artificially, checking me out as though searching for a plug to pull which would deflate me and so do the universe a favour. I don't know why she so obviously despised me. Perhaps because I'm a Natural.

The Walrus humphed impatiently, snout flapping.

"Right," said Stacker, "to business." His elbow grinned nastily. "Fancy yourself perky on a board, my son?"

The Walrus gave a wet guffaw.

"He does," agreed Beluga. "So we come to make him the offer he cannot throw up."

"You wanna make some quick money?" Stacker nodded, agreeing with himself, so that he resembled a pair of giraffes in combat. "He does. Perhaps enough to get some real muscles on them scrawny bones." A couple of drawers popped open and sent him gliding across the stellar surface, uncomfortably close to me.

"Now listen to this. All you have to do is take a little trip on that board you're so good with, and do us a teensy tiny errand. Sound good?"

"Deliver a message?" I asked, leaning away from him.

Beluga leaned on her board and drifted to my other side, so that leaning away from Stacker was now impossible without getting a faceful of Beluga. She laughed. "No," she said. "Just tap on the ship." She pretended to tap on my chest with one appalled finger.

I began to laugh myself. Out of hysteria, because The Walrus was now towering over me, dribbling, tiny eyes wide. And out of disbelief. Everyone knows that skinnies can't possibly make real contact with the universe, let alone tap on a spaceship. The most you can do is surf on the stars. For real contact you need massive cryochip computers, like the Intergalactic Transport Corporation has. Otherwise everybody would be flitting by themselves from colony to colony between the stars, and wouldn't need the ITC.

"It's a genuine offer," Beluga said. "We have worked out a way for young skinnies, such as you and I, to have some impact on the universe."

"Yeah," said Stacker. "Try it. You got nothing to lose." He reached into one drawer with the foot on his head and produced a wad of credit slips.

Beluga took them from him and waved them beneath my chin, looking cynical.

The Walrus groaned expectantly, flapping his jowls.

I was tempted. Already I had thoughts of a goose flensing attachment for my ZX4900.

"Just there and back?"

"Won't take a jiffy for a quick lad like you," Stacker's middle thigh told me.

"You'll be fabulous," said Beluga.

The Walrus hooted admiringly.

The mixture of contempt and flattery got to me, I guess.

"Okay," I said.

"Right," said Stacker. "Now, there's just one little requirement ..."

"What's that?"

"I think we should get someone else," said Beluga. "He's not ready for this thing. Too squeamish. Too stupid."

"Leave the boy alone," Stacker told her. To me he said, "Don't worry, it's not dangerous or painful. I done it myself thousands of times. You're not squeamish are you?"

"Well, not really ..."

"I got to warn you, it doesn't look nice," said Stacker.

"But once you get over that, it's dreaming," said Beluga.

"Don't you mean dreamy?" I asked.

"You correct me, Nature boy?" she snapped. "Let's go," she said to the others.

The Walrus nodded, tusks touching his chest.

"No, no, I'll do it! What do I have to do?" I asked.

"You suck this," said Stacker.

And out of another drawer he pulled a paper package.

Inside the package were slugs.

WHAT TO DO IF:

• *You get lost or feel vertigo. Don't worry. Just release the grips to quit to your normal state, and don't save your location. (See* Saving the Universe, *Fig. 42.)*

• *Total meltdown occurs. Seek immediate medical assistance. Do not scream.*

Straight away I let go of the handles. I mean, really – slugs? Or at least I tried to let go. Beluga grabbed my hands with hers.

"You – you touched me!"

"Of course I touched you, idiot. That's what we've just now been talking about!"

"Here, give it a try," said Stacker, thrusting the package beneath my chin.

The slugs roamed peacefully, gracefully even, around the plastic box inside the wrapping. I could not let go, I could not move away, at least not unless I took Beluga with me.

"Are you going to force me?"

The slugs glistened, white and orange and spotted peacock

blue, rippling over one another, closer now, right by my lips.

The Walrus chortled at my expression. Grey flesh slapped against itself, the reports coming like gunshots both through my hands and Beluga's. He flung back his head, revealing shark-like rows of decaying teeth.

Then I realised:

Beluga had her hands off the grips. It was simply impossible. Any number of fail-safes ensured you'd revert back to normal state if you let go.

"So now you know, Nature boy. I do not go back. I am most skinny person of all time. I have eaten so many slugs you cannot imagine. Sucking is not sufficient. I live on them." She laughed delightedly, took one and swallowed it whole, like an oyster, and licked the slime off her lips. I realised now what the silver trails on her chin were. "We will not make you if you are too stupid to see where the future lies." Her inky skin rippled like night water in a breeze.

To prove her point she let go of me.

Now, I could have left then. But what did they want me to do? Tap on a spaceship. No big deal.

Except for the part about sucking slugs.

With one hand I pushed Stacker's package away from me. "Why do you want to do this anyway? And why can't you do it yourselves?"

Stacker dropped a pair of green lips into my hand, remotes. "We're freedom fighters. The ITC has dominated the spaceways for too long! Ordinary people want to take their share of the riches on the frontier planets as well. And that's who we're for: ordinary people. So what do you say? Join us!"

The lips fizzed dramatically and disappeared in a flash of light.

He had a point. Everyone knew it, but the ITC were too powerful. Anyone who annoyed them they just bought out. I examined the three with fresh eyes. Stacker still looked shifty, but then with so many stray parts it was unavoidable. Beluga's scorn for my kind fell into place. The Walrus was motionless with expectation.

Stacker offered me the package, more gently now.

I reached in and took out a slug. I knew that if I hesitated it would never make it to my mouth, so I brought it squirming towards me and just pushed it inside.

The slug writhed on my tongue.

"Eueeechchch!" I spat and spat and still felt slimy. I couldn't tell if my nausea was from the taste or its effect. "Yick! Ptui! Bletch!"

As soon as I had subsided a bit Stacker said, "Now, quick!"

I nodded, still grimacing, distracted. Where had the slug gone? Something felt suspicious down my shirt.

He pointed with one leg. "That way, and stop just after the blue giant. The starliner will be obvious, it's so big. All you have to do is tap on its side three times near the rear plasma ventricle and you will have done your part."

Tapping near the ventricle. Now where had I heard of that?

"Go!" said Stacker. "There's no time to lose!"

Before I leaned on my board I glanced at Beluga. She stuffed the wad of credit slips in my pocket and began to chuckle.

As I glided off her laughter rang cruelly through my bones.

I have to admit they were right about me. I am a born skinny. I soared certainly through the uncertain universe. And it was truly beautiful: the stars and gases were coloured so delicately, scattered so elegantly and over such a magnificent expanse that I forgot my nerves, even my revulsion.

But only for a while. Beluga's laughter perplexed me. It was more than a laugh of revolutionary triumph; it was sadistic, self-interested. I might be serving their cause, but there had to be some hidden delight for her in my touching a spaceship, some danger. Probably to do with its more intense form of attenuat –

Tapping near the plasma ventricle!

Now I recalled where I had heard of it. The other week a liner had imploded. All its passengers were now microscopic and had to be kept in a jar because of a mysterious malfunction of the plasma ventricle. Forensic experts had attributed it to an interstellar dust particle locked in a natural state of partial attenuation after the Big Bang, a time when the whole universe had been attenuated.

But I knew better. Some poor slug-sucker had done the "freedom fighters'" dirty work for them.

Well, no way was I going to jail for them. Especially not when I had found something (at last) that I was good at.

So what to do about the intergalactic slug-suckers?

I leaned to my right, made a complete turn, skipped and stopped. I would never find them now; they'd have left. The universe was a big place. There was nothing I could do except let go of my handles and tell the authorities. So I let go.

Nothing happened.

It took a while for my situation to impact. I could not go back. I would stay attenuated until my body starved to death – or more likely I'd stay on a drip, vegetable for life – back in the real world.

I panicked. I positively raced to the ship I was supposed to sabotage and scooted around in front of its scanners, waving like a dill and yelling, "Hey you! Stop! Yoo-hoo! Look! I'm out here and I can't get back. Please, notice me!" They did not pick me up. Naturally. They were much, much more attenuated than I was, by huge attenuation generators, even if I had sucked some slimy mollusc. So I watched the liner cruise into the brilliant green distance.

I let go of my handles again. I tried to think fat. Only my knees vanished and entered the real world. I had never known I had fat knees. But no matter how hard I tried, I could not get any further. The same thing must have happened to the nostril person, I realised. And even when I had pulled him through it had not done him any good. So I gave up on that one. I jumped off the board and watched it float away. Then I was consumed by a terror of spending eternity in infinite space with not even a virtual board to cling to, and I grabbed the handles again.

I had to think. I was thin, attenuated, sub-molecular (even if stars seemed little things to me); I might be able to enter the electronic world of the attenuating device itself and pass a message on through its software. I tried to think myself into the handles beneath my palms.

Nothing happened.

So that was that. My last possibility. I was stuck here. I have to tell you, I cried like a baby.

This lasted for a good while. I had all the time in the universe, after all. But I did begin to think again, about what a nong I had been.

And something moved between my singlet and shirt.

I reached for it.

It was the slug. Half-sucked, but living. It curled and foamed when I poked it.

A slug. Perhaps it would alter my attenuation if I sucked some more. Perhaps I might try the world of electrons again. How had they known to suck slugs anyhow? I wondered. They must have tried all kinds of things at random, possibly worse things. They really were weirdos.

I realised I was stalling. I had to suck that slug. I closed my eyes, pinched my nose and popped the slug into my mouth, thinking as thin and electron-y as I could.

Here I am. Just me and the slug. (I've called it Orlando.) When I didn't return to my own body and my parents went insane with alarm, the experts came and checked the software, and hopefully now I'm either in their computers or in some other attenuware into which they've downloaded me in the name of saving me.

Perhaps I'm in several pieces of software.

When I think about it, if I'm in some piece of software (could I have been copied?), then I'm a virus. Fancy that.

I'm swimming in a blue world full of bubbles, and the bubbles go where I push them, and I push them to make words.

Hey, if I can make words, maybe someone is reading this! And if you are –

Please help me.

```
pppp   l     eeee       a           ssss
p  p   l     e           a a        s  s
p  p   l      e          a a        s
pppp   l      eee      aaaa          ss
p      l      e       a   a            s
p      l       e     a     aa          s
p      l       e     a       a         s
p      llll    eeee  a                 s
                                      s
                                       s
                                        
                                        s
                                         s
                                         s

                                       pleass hel
```

VIRUS DETECTED! ANTI-VIRAL RUNNING! VIRUS DETECTED! ANTI-VIRAL RUNNING! VIRUS DETECTED!

HyperCoric *takes no responsibility for any person or equipment damaged by continued use after statutory warnings. Users with corrupted attenuware should destroy (by fire) the infected disks and have all other exposed components scanned, hospitalised and, if necessary, repaired (at the user's expense), by an authorised dealer.*

– T Stacker, Hygiene Operations

Afterword

Scientifically, this story is implausible, I know – I revel in that. Which is one reason to write SF (pronounced "soof"): the future will always turn out stranger than we think. What I see as the more solid SF content of "Malcolm", though, is its look at the way we read and write science and technology. We are surrounded by fiction masquerading as various kinds of fact. It's often said that history books are fiction, we are persuaded by the writer's shifts of emphasis and identification with particular personalities, by the writer's rhythm and tone, that events happened this way or that. Well, one role of instruction manuals is to convince the appliance user that no matter what happens, they have bought the right gadget. Also, that anything that does go wrong with the gadget is not the maker's fault.

Smells suspiciously like rewriting history to me, except in advance.

You can make a case for this being true of all sorts of writing, even scientific kinds. When you apply to other writing the skills you learn as a reader of fiction, it helps you see through the "facts" to the advertising and propaganda underneath. Hopefully, that will help you use the gadget or understand the science better as well.

Circles of Fire

Sophie Masson

Sophie Masson *was born in Jakarta, Indonesia, in 1959, and came to Australia with her parents, who are both French, in 1963. She was brought up in Sydney but left to live in the country when she was about twenty-one.*

Her first story was published in the Newcastle Herald *in 1985, and her first story in an anthology in 1988 (in* After Dark, *compiled by Gillian Rubinstein and published by Omnibus Books). Her first book,* The House in the Rainforest, *came out in 1990. Since then she has had several books published, her most recent being* The Cousin from France *(1993).*

She lives near Armidale, New South Wales, in a mudbrick house with her husband and three children.

The first sign came with the blazing onset of an early summer. Every day the sun shone out of a sky that looked as if it had been applied with thick metallic paint. Every day we heard the announcer on the radio say, "There is no rain forecast, for today or for the near future."

At first no one worried too much. The weather was just right to bring all the wheat and corn to bursting-head stage. It was eerie, really, I suppose: you could drive from one end of the country to the other and see the grain, shivering like a golden-green skin over the darkness of the land. Hardly any animals; they took up too much room, you see. Millions had been slaughtered, their bodies bulldozed into mass graves. We'd had to kill lots of sheep; Mum hadn't liked it much, but Dad had said there was no help for it: the future was based on grain. There was even talk of a new process developed by scientists – a process that could turn the beautiful golden straw of the harvest into fabrics. The Rumpelstiltskin process, it was called. We'd seen pictures of the fabric on TV. It was amazing, just like a rustling, living gold.

There were many more people living in the inland now, because of the rise in the sea-level. There hadn't been any proper planning, though, because the government had waited until the last minute, and so ugly shanty-towns made of bright corrugated iron had sprung up everywhere. In that year, in that summer, the air was filled with the soft glow of grain and the harsh sun-glare of corrugated iron. Sun, iron, grain: a fierce panoply of gold and silver, shining to the ends of the land.

Like so many farmers, Dad mistrusted the settlement dwellers. "Why do those people live like that, huddling together like animals, instead of like us?" he said once. He was looking out beyond our crops as he spoke, towards the shanty-town. You could see the roofs winking, even from here. But Mum had sighed. "Poor folks," she'd said, mysteriously, and she'd turned back to the cool green interior of our house, and to the books she was always reading. Dad said she read too much, the wrong kind of books – mythology, legends, even the Bible. I loved my mother, but I couldn't even begin to understand her thinking.

The harvest was just about to start. Dad had organised all sorts of people to come and work, and he'd even gone to the settlement to find extra workers. But he'd come home from *there* in a bad temper. "Those people!" he said to Mum and me. "Don't know how to work. Spend their days inside watching TV! One fellow even rambled on at me about some story he'd heard, about circles that had been *burnt*, if you please, into the crops of farmers overseas! I tell you, those people will believe anything!"

But that night, when we turned on the TV, the presenter of the News, with an apologetic lilt to his voice, told us that circles had begun appearing in grain crops on the other side of the country. It was unprecedented – everyone knew that the news was nothing but economics now. Any other kind was self-indulgent, we were told.

Dad grumbled about it as we went to bed. "Circles indeed,"

he said, but he looked a little shaken at the inclusion of such a story in his sacrosanct News.

Mum said nothing. There was a look on her face, a watching kind of look I'd never seen before. Watching and listening; as if there was something in the air that she could glimpse but not quite understand.

The next day, the sky was exactly the same – thick, glossy, deep blue, the sun exploding quietly up there millions of kilometres above us. Dad wasn't at breakfast. That wasn't surprising, because it was the first day of the harvest, and normally he'd be off very early. But Mum wasn't there either, and I was surprised by that, because at harvest time she worked constantly in the kitchen, baking cakes for the workers. I wandered around looking for her, but she wasn't anywhere in the house. Finally I saw her standing on the veranda, stock still, staring out at the paddocks. I came up to her and said, sleepily, hoping to make her feel motherly so she'd bustle about to make me some breakfast: "Mum, where do we keep the coffee?"

My plaintive voice didn't seem to reach her, so I repeated it, more loudly. Still she said nothing. So I said, still more loudly, "*Mum!* Where do we – "

She turned around to me then, and her look was chilling. "Look, Deborah," she said. "Look out there."

In front of us were those beautiful waving oceans of grain that we'd looked at every day. Except that, as far as the eye could see, symmetrical circles had been cut – no, *burnt* – into the grain. There was something terrifying about the perfect charred circles, black on gold and green. Paddock after paddock they spread, geometrically perfect, tonnes of grain burnt off just at its harvest fullness.

"Oh *no*," I whispered.

Mum said nothing. She just stood and gazed at the grain, as if she could see the future.

I looked at her cautiously. "What did Dad say?"

"What do you *think*," she snapped. Then she spoke more gently. "He's gone to see the neighbours, to see if it's happened there ..." She paused, shaded her eyes. "I always thought something like this would happen one day. We were always so sure we were right, so *merciless* in our rightness."

I stared at her. Had the whole thing unhinged her? She walked slowly back inside the house, and I followed her, theorising at the top of my voice. "Probably some wind effect," I said. "Or a sun spot. Or some effect of the hole in the ozone." Mum paid no attention. She went over to the bookcase in the corner of the living-room and pulled out a book.

"Maybe it's vandals," I continued. "From the settlement. Armed with blowtorches."

Mum didn't answer. She opened the book. I couldn't understand it. She was shocked, I decided kindly. Shock took people in funny ways.

"Mum," I reminded her. "Shouldn't you be making cakes and things? The workers will be here soon."

"There'll be no harvest," said Mum. She said it flatly, as if it wasn't a complete heresy.

"Don't be silly!" I said. "Of course there will be!"

"It's only the beginning," Mum said, sadly. She put the book down on the table. "They'll be back."

"Who? The vandals? Oh no," I said. "The government's well-organised. They'll find out who's responsible. They'll make arrests."

Mum looked at me. "But why should the settlement people burn our crops?" she said, even more sadly.

"They don't need a reason," I said. "They're thick. They're

not like us. You know that!"

Mum shook her head and walked away, out to the kitchen. I was going to follow her, to get my cup of coffee, when I looked at the book she'd left lying on the table. To my astonishment, it was my old copy of the Bible, which I used to love because it was illustrated with all kinds of dramatic, rich pictures. It was a big book, heavy. I opened it up, and flicked through the pages. There were Noah and his family on the ark, riding high above the flood that destroyed the world; Adam and Eve in the Garden of Eden; Moses parting the Red Sea; and the angels – Michael, Gabriel, Raphael, Azrael and the others.

The picture of the angels had always impressed me – they were not benign Christmas card beings with white wings and golden hair, but fierce and fiery, with eyes that flamed red and gold, and wheels of fire at their sides. I read the caption under them, a passage taken from the book of Ezekiel: "They had the form of men, but with four faces, fire flashing forth continually. Their legs were straight, the soles of their feet sparkled like burnished bronze. And I saw a wheel upon the earth, one for each of them, the rims of the wheels full of eyes round about ..." This was fire personified, like the sun come to Earth, like a force of nature neither controllable nor understandable.

A cold shiver rippled over me as I looked at the picture. Then I closed the book and put it gently back in the bookcase.

When Dad came home, he was wound tighter than an alarm clock. "They're everywhere, those circles," he announced tersely to Mum. "The crops are ruined."

Immediately – would you believe it? – my mother began to protest, saying that of course the crops weren't ruined, that they could save quite a bit of them, and that she was sure there was a good explanation for it all.

"It's not that," Dad said. "You don't understand. All the grain has been ruined, not only what was burnt, but all the other plants too – all the ears are empty, there's only husks hanging there. It's weird – as if the grain has been pulled out from the inside."

Mum and Dad looked at each other for a long moment, then Dad said, quickly, "Ah well, the police are on to it. It's obviously the work of some crazies from the settlement." There was something hard and brilliant about his eyes as he said this, something that caught at my throat.

The police came, and took notes and photographs. One policeman, the senior one, said, "It's been happening all over the country, you know. It must be a really devilish organisation, a most efficient one." He smiled, as if the idea of such a monstrous enemy filled him with a harsh joy.

"We'll find them, never fear," he went on. "People like that ... hardly people at all. More like ... like animals."

I had a sudden memory of a sheep we used to have, years ago, when you were allowed to keep animals. It had been a nuisance, that one; it never wanted to stay in a mob, and so it had ended up in the freezer. Gold eyes, it had, alien eyes, with strange pupils. I had refused to eat its flesh. I wasn't sure why. Just as I wasn't sure why the policeman's words should evoke in me such a memory. Or such a shiver.

The police didn't find the organisation. Not that week or the next, or the one after that. People in the settlement were stopped and searched, lots of arrests were made, and because the situation was so serious, the government suspended civil rights – just for a few weeks.

But still the circles kept appearing, charring and ruining crops everywhere. Soon martial law was proclaimed, and the settlements were put under curfew, while hectares and hectares of dead grain crops shrivelled in the sun. There was not even enough straw to salvage for the Rumpelstiltskin process. The news from overseas was just the same.

Still the sun kept shining out of the corrugated blue sky, still its brazen eye engulfed us in rays of heat. Mum spent nearly all her time either on the veranda, scanning the sky; or in her chair in the living-room, staring into space. Once, I came in to ask her something, and I heard her muttering, "Mercy ... we *do* know mercy," and it was odd, it was as if she were pleading with someone, someone unseen. I *knew* she was going mad. I felt on the brink of madness myself. It was this sun, this endless, endless blue sky.

And then the killings began. A settlement boy, returning late from a day spent illegally outside his iron walls, was shot by a farmer. A family sneaking out under cover of darkness to raid someone's vegetable garden; a girl who'd been found scrawling graffiti – these and others were shot. Most people we knew thought it a sad necessity. Dad said, "You know, we're at war here. At war with a most terrible organisation, diabolically cunning."

Mum said nothing. She hadn't said anything for a long time, come to think of it.

As for me, well, I didn't know what to think. On TV, I'd seen a few of those settlement faces: lean and pale, with uneven features and coarse hair, their eyes filled with hate. They spoke badly and ranted and looked as though they smelled. They looked like undesirables, like people who for some twisted reason of their own would hold the whole country, the whole world, to ransom. I remembered one in particular, a woman they later executed: remembered the look in her eyes as she said, "Soon the trumpets will sound, there will be fire, blood!" Her eyes were shining as she looked straight at the camera, at us; a kind of triumph that seemed to fill every pore of her skin shone out from her. And I'd thought, with a shudder: yes, they *are* dangerous, they hate us, they must be destroyed! But sometimes, I wondered. Was it really possible that they possessed a power stronger than hunger, fear, or death? Were they really so unlike us?

Then, one day, quite simply, there were no more circles. But executions became even more commonplace, and curfew laws were tightened: settlement people were absolutely forbidden to venture outside their walls – at any time.

"We have to do this," Dad said. "You know that. It's them or us – them or us."

"It's always been like that," Mum said sadly. "There never is understanding. Perhaps the understanding cannot even be allowed. No, we will get no mercy. We can expect none." She got up from where she'd been sitting, and the book she'd been reading slid off her lap. She walked to the window and looked at the unchanging sky.

I picked up the book: it was my old Bible, open at Revelations. And with a shock of horror I recognised the words: "The first angel blew his trumpet, and there followed hail and fire, mixed with blood, which fell on the earth; and a third of the earth was burnt up, and the trees, and all the green grass was burnt up ..." I remembered the hate in that settlement woman's eyes; I remembered how the Old Testament angels had been God's executioners, the messengers of righteous punishment, the avengers of the meek and oppressed. I shivered as I looked at those angel faces, rigid with rightness: a force as unyielding and terrifying as the sun. Such faces would show no mercy, I knew that. And the wheels of fire, by the angels' side, did they not remind me of something? Of something perfect yet frightening, something that should not have been there, but was: circles in the crops. *Burnt in.* Circles of fire, all over the land. They had been a warning to us – but we had not understood. Because no one ever understood. The judgement had been made. Now we could only wait.

"We need rain," Dad said loudly. "Rain, to wash away this madness." Nobody answered him. Nobody spoke. Not even when the fire sirens began, long and wailing and distant at first.

Afterword

I realised for the first time that science fiction needn't mean technical nightmares and incomprehensible jargon about hardware when I began to read the work of Ray Bradbury. Here was something I could relate to – human dilemmas, shadowy borderlands where reality and fantasy merge, the strangeness inside the human psyche that leads us to make monsters and aliens out of each other. After the inevitable Tolkien phase, I wasn't much taken with swords and sorcery, or high fantasy – although my very first attempt at a novel did indeed blend all kinds of mythologies (it was never published, and I've kept it as a salutary reminder in my bottom drawer!).

Nearly all my books have incorporated a slice of those borderlands, for I think the world is much stranger, much more complex – and yet much simpler – than it looks. "Circles of Fire", though, is my first published science fiction story – if by science fiction one means an alternative view of reality, a reality pushed to its limits, and then just that bit further.

The idea first came to me at the height of the crop circles phenomenon in the UK, the whole thing fascinated me, even though subsequently it was all revealed to be a hoax. At the time, I was also re-reading the Bible with greater interest than before, finding it far stranger, far more disconcerting, than I'd thought. The angels fascinated me most of all. The idea I'd had of them as a child was not at all what was described in the Bible; these were creatures of fire and flame, with molten bodies and a thousand eyes. With a shiver of delight and unease, I recognised in the angels of Ezekiel and Revelations ... the aliens. Here were the seeds, it seemed to me, of all those strange, relentless, inhuman creatures beloved of a certain kind of science fiction. I played around with dozens of ideas before being able to combine the two.

Science fiction is a means of voyaging to the margins as well as the core; by layering ancient and modern in "Circles of Fire", I integrated both. For while we look towards the stars, and watch for future generations in UFOs, the core of ourselves remains as we were thousands of years ago, when those extraordinary Middle Eastern nomads first conceived the body of imaginative, fierce and powerful literature we know as the Bible.

ABOUT THE AUTHORS

Lucy Sussex was born in 1957, in Christchurch, New Zealand, and has travelled widely. She writes in various areas, from children's literature to science fiction to the detective genre, and has an interest in rediscovering and reprinting the work of nineteenth-century women writers. She has published one children's novel, *The Peace Garden*, and another, for teenagers, *Deersnake*. In addition, she has published a collection of short stories, *My Lady Tongue & Other Tales*. When not writing or editing, she works as a researcher.

• ——————— •• ——————— •

Gary Crew was born in 1947 in Brisbane, Queensland, and still lives there today. He lectures in Creative Writing at Queensland University of Technology and holds a Masters degree in Commonwealth Literature from the University of Queensland. At present he is writing full time with the assistance of a Category A Fellowship from the Australia Council Literature Board.

Gary Crew is the author of five novels: *The Inner Circle*, *The House of Tomorrow*, *Strange Objects*, *No Such Country*, and *Angel's Gate*. His picture books include *First Light* (illustrated by Peter Gouldthorpe), *Tracks*, and *Lucy's Bay* (both illustrated by Gregory Rogers). His short stories are represented in several anthologies.

In 1991 *Strange Objects* won the Children's Book Council of Australia's Book of the Year (Older Readers) Award, the Alan Marshall Prize for Children's Literature, and the NSW Premier's Award for Children's Literature; and more recently it has been shortlisted for the Edgar Allan Poe Award for Mystery Fiction in the USA. *Angel's Gate* won the National Children's Book Award in the 1994 Adelaide Festival Awards for Literature.

Rick Kennett was born in 1956 in Melbourne and has lived there ever since (he hates to travel). When he left school at fifteen, he was already scribbling SF-ish stories in exercise books. He endured eight years in various engineering jobs, for which he was ill-suited, and attended the Terry Carr/George Turner science fiction writers' workshop in 1979. He left the course half way through and published his first story a month later. Since then he has had several stories published in both UK and Australian small press and in several anthologies. Between 1985 and 1991 he hosted a science fiction show on Melbourne public radio. He became a motorcycle courier in 1980 and has not looked back.

• ——————— •• ——————— •

Isobelle Carmody was born in Wangaratta and moved to Melbourne soon afterwards. The eldest of eight children, she began her first book, *Obernewtyn*, while still at secondary school. She studied Philosophy and Drama at University, then worked as a features journalist and later as a radio interviewer. *Obernewtyn*, and its sequel, *The Farseekers*, were both shortlisted for the CBC Book of the Year Award in the Older Readers category, while her third book, *Scatterlings*, won the Talking Book of the Year Award. Her most recent novel, *The Gathering*, was joint winner of the Children's Literature Peace Prize in 1993.

• ——————— •• ——————— •

Sean McMullen is a computer analyst with the Bureau of Meteorology, and lives in Melbourne with his wife and daughter. He is a graduate of the University of Melbourne where he is still an instructor with the university karate club, and he has played and sung in several bands. He has had over two dozen SF stories published in Australia, Britain, and the USA and has twice won the Australian Ditmar Award for science fiction. His first book, *Call to the Edge*, was published in 1992, and his novel *Voices in the Light* in 1994.

Mustafa Zahirovic is twenty-four years old, lives in Melbourne, and is a physiotherapist. He says: "Over the past couple of years I have been treating my writing more seriously and my first professional sale now appears on the inside of a tram somewhere. I have yet to see it, but apparently it's read by commuters daily.

"As well as short stories I enjoy writing poetry and film scripts. I hope to explore all these interests further and to complete a novel in the near future. I am encouraged by the success of my shorter fiction, which has been printed in both professional and small-press magazines in Australia and overseas."

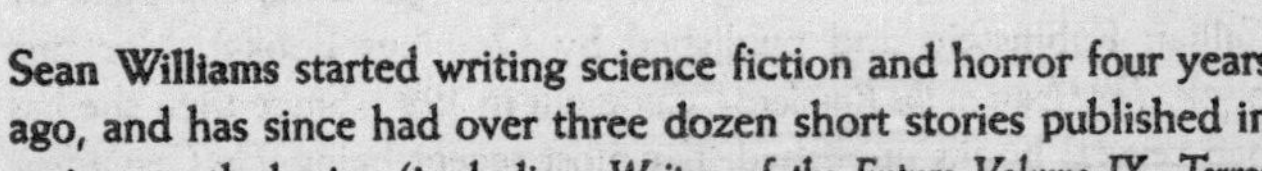

Sean Williams started writing science fiction and horror four years ago, and has since had over three dozen short stories published in various anthologies (including *Writers of the Future Volume IX*, *Terror Australis*, and *Intimate Armageddons*) and magazines (*Aboriginal SF*, *Bloodsongs*, *Aurealis*, *Eidolon*, *EOD*, and others). He is co-author, with Shane Dix, of the first three novels of the *Cogal* series.

When not writing, he pursues his other major hobby (music) by working in a compact disc shop, studying part-time, and collecting the works of the late Frank Zappa. He was born in Whyalla and currently lives in Adelaide (which he destroys every now and again, just to relieve tension).

Paul Voermans is Dutch-Indonesian. He was born in Gippsland in 1960 and currently lives in Melbourne again after several years abroad. At sixteen he attended a science fiction writers' workshop during the school holidays; and his first science fiction story, written there, was published in *The View from the Edge*, edited by George Turner. Since then his stories have appeared in both Australian and English magazines. His two science fiction novels, *And Disregards the Rest* and *The Weird Colonial Boy*, are published by Victor Gollancz,

London. He has ten years' experience as an actor, including a lead role in the ABC TV series *Trapp, Winkle and Box*, and has exhibited performance masks at the National Gallery of Victoria and taught mime at the Victorian College of the Arts. Fish fascinate him.

• ———————— •• ———————— •

Sophie Masson was born in Jakarta, Indonesia, in 1959, and came to Australia with her parents, who are both French, in 1963. She was brought up in Sydney but left to live in the country when she was about twenty-one.

Her first story was published in the *Newcastle Herald* in 1985, and her first story in an anthology in 1988 (in *After Dark*, compiled by Gillian Rubinstein and published by Omnibus Books). Her first book, *The House in the Rainforest*, came out in 1990. Since then she has had several books published, her most recent being *The Cousin from France* (1993).

She lives near Armidale, New South Wales, in a mudbrick house with her husband and three children.